Queen's Up

By:

CityBoy 4rm Dade

Copyright © 2018 Soulja Choc Presents

All rights reserved. Without limiting the rights under copyright reserved. No part of this book may be reproduced, stored in any or introduced into a retrieval system, to transmitted in any form, or by any means (Electronic, mechanical, photocopying, recording, or otherwise), without prior written consent from both the author and the publisher, except for the brief quotes that are used in literary reviews.

This is a work of fiction. It is not meant to depict, portray or represent any particular real persons. All the characters, incidents and dialogues are the product of the author's imagination and are not to be construed as real. Any references or similarities to actual events, entities, real people (living or dead) or to real locales and/or to any particular places of locations are only intended to give the novel a sense of actuality and reality. Any similarity in names, characters, entities and incidents is and are absolutely coincidental.

1st Published by: Soulja Choc Presents on 08/20/2018

ISBN used on CreateSpace

9781726003483

CAUTION !!!!

Even adults must review the contents with extreme caution due to the graphic sexual and extremely violent content

Dedication and Acknowledgments

This work of art is dedicated to all the fallen soldiers who fell victim to the struggle, whether six feet under or confined behind the walls of the penitentiary. They said I couldn't do it, said I wouldn't make it. Now look, I'm a manifestation of greatness. I didn't find this talent, it somehow found me!

I was once told to build my own dreams, or someone else would hire me to build theirs. Even from prison with a confinement pen, a few packs of paper and couple of hours of free time, I've managed to construct a book that will help me to never throw rocks at the chain gang again.

Special thanks goes to Christopher Hamilton and Kenniesha Turner, you both never gave up on me and told me that I had 3 choices; to give up, give in or give it all I have and look at me now.

I hold four hands at the poker table.

You encouraged me when my circumstances and environment left me discouraged. You believed in me when I didn't know what to believe. So to my readers, fans, and friends; let this be motivation for those with sight but no vision.

You should be your biggest fan, we all will die one day the goal isn't to live forever. The goal is to create something that will live forever. None of us can make a brand new start but we can start to make a brand new ending….

Asalaamu' Wa'lakium Rahmatualluh

CityBoy

Prologue

Alexus and her younger sister Mercedes were slowly making a name for themselves in the gruesome streets of Miami. Thanks to their father who showed them the ins and outs of the streets ever since they were old enough to remember. They watched him cook crack-cocaine, buy it, weigh it, and sell it. Their father, Sampson took them with him a few times to meet his suppliers too. He occasionally hosted casual dinners with lawyers, judges, dirty cops, and corrupt federal agents that he paid for immunity and protection.

At the time, Alexus and Mercedes didn't understand what was really going on but they admired the respect, loyalty, and honor among everyone. Their father introduced them to members of his "business circle" and showed them who to be on the lookout for because all smiles aren't real and all handshakes aren't friendly.

You may think that Sampson trained his daughters for the street life, but it was the complete opposite. He never intended for them to get involved in the game, he just wanted them to know of it.

Alexus and Mercedes had different plans.

After years of watching their father orchestrate an empire, they felt that the street life was a part of them and they took it all in. As serious as a heart attack they trained day and night from the gun range to the projects.

Two years prior they stole a key of cocaine from their dad and started a street team called Queens Up. The clique turned out to be pretty successful because Alexus and Mercedes both had an eye for loyalty, respect and honor thanks to the example set by their dad.

Kenya was from the Back Blues in Opa-Locka. The government assisted apartments where she grew up was notoriously known for sex, money and murder. She was raised by the hood, no dad and a drug addicted prostitute for a mother.

Kenya never experienced a childhood as a result of being left with all the parental responsibility of her two younger brothers. During her free time she had cousins she vibed with, who were deeply rooted in the streets. To make ends meet she ran minor errands for her cousins until she met Alexus at the Uncle Al Festival in the heart of Liberty City.

Alexus knew the moment that she vibed with Kenya that she was built Ford tough and would fit perfectly on her team.

Then there was Jordan, he had been gay since about middle school but he wasn't feminine. He played the dominant role in all his relationships. If you didn't know Jordan you would never suspect him of being gay. He wasn't on the down low, he was very comfortable with his sexual preference.

Jordan jumped off the porch in Coconut Grove but was originally from Carol City, He had recently turned 24 and had already left a couple women childless. Although Jordan was gay he was about his issue and knew how to make a dollar out of a penny and a plan; all he needed was a little guidance.

Last summer at Club Boulevard he exchanged words with some niggas from a clique called Str8Drop. They were ruthless and feared throughout the hoods of Miami. Three of them jumped Jordan but it happened that Mercedes was also in the club that night. She had watched the whole thing go down and because Jordan was ten toes down and didn't back away she decided to be in his corner.

Mercedes pulled out her .380 and shot at the two of them while Jordan pulled his switch blade and stabbed the other one in the chest, sending him crashing to the floor. Since then a bond was formed and they never looked back.

That's how Queens Up came about.

Although Alexus and Mercedes were sitting on thirty six ounces of the purest cocaine since the 80's, they didn't put their plans in motion just yet. They took their time getting to know their new crew members for about three months then right when they thought the perfect time had come, shit went sour.

1

Zetta

When I opened the door I was greeted by the luxurious living room and immediately inhaled the scent of marijuana as if I had the joint dangling from my lips.

There were pictures of Bob Marley on every wall. On an elegant entertainment stand sat a 72 inch Plasma TV with a big ass Jamaican flag behind it.

No one was in the living room but I already knew that because Diamond told me they would be in his bedroom. I quietly eased the front door shut and crept down the hall gun in hand.

Hearing soft laughter let me know which room they were in.

Diamond and I have been in the game now for about a year and half now. Altogether it took me about six months to break her in before she was up to date with her talk game and mentally point enough to talk a fish onto a fish hook.

I remember our very first heist together. This dumb bitch almost got us killed but I stay on point and was one step ahead of the lames. That one false move was enough to convince her that mistakes will get her weave dyed red. She been on point since then and she's perfecting the acting part of this shit.

When I first met Diamond I didn't see just a bad Puerto Rican bitch I saw potential, hunger and opportunity. I knew she wasn't gay but I put my bid in anyway. It took some time for me to break her but I was up for the challenge when I saw how niggas were really on her trail. That's when I laced her with the game.

Diamond is five foot seven inches tall about 140 pounds of pure ass, hips and thighs with no stomach. She had the prettiest white teeth, shoulder length hair and blueish green eyes. A couple of niggas was in her chest but not like me, I'm a female so I know what hoes desire.

I heard Diamond telling Dread that she had to go to the bathroom, bringing me back to reality, I had zoned out for a second. I pushed the room door open and Dread was reclined on the King sized bed smoking a big ass spliff.

"Who the bumboclat you my youth?" he started to ask but I cut him off.

"Shut the fuck up, you know what time it is! Get on the floor right now and don't try no slick shit!" I said seriously, but not trying to talk more than I needed to.

"Easy dat gal don't shoot me now ya hear? Just tell me what me can do fa you!"

"You can give me the combination to the safe!" Diamond said while stepping out of the bathroom.

"Bloodclaut you ah'sheet me up! You'sa dead gal!"

I slapped him with the barrel of my Glock 40, bringing his attention to the reality of the situation and opening up his skull in the process. He screamed in pain as blood dripped down his face. "Where that check at Dread?" Don't play no games! We know this spot because we watched you bring money here four times!" I told him, cocking back to slap him with my gun again.

"I'mma ask you one time and Dread…. Before you answer remember, whateva in that safe you can get back but if I take yo life its gone foreva and whether you live or die the safe is still leaving with me."

Diamond walked in the closet where the safe was.

"So what its going be rude boy!?" I asked, anxious to give him a permanent part in his head if he said the wrong thing.

"Take all of dat ya hear? Just leave me wit my life! The numba is 2-28-22!" he said apparently scared to death.

"It's open!" yelled Diamond from the closet.

"Good" I said to him and her at the same time, "You know what to do bae!"

After she finished emptying the safe into one of Dread's Adidas duffel bags I squeezed the trigger of my Glock twice sending Dread to either sip champagne with God or shoot heroine with the devil. Diamond got the gallon of bleach from the bathroom and poured it all throughout the room. After leaving a pound of weed by the head of Dread's lifeless body, we made a quick but careful exit.

When we got in the car and pulled out of Dread's driveway, Diamond kissed my cheek and rubbed her hand up and down my thighs, then she whispered in my ear and gently bit me on the ear lobe. We made it back to our lil duck off at about 5:30 am and counted everything we had hit Dread for, which was 26 thousand dollars in cash and 3 pounds of some grade "A" mango kush.

    Filled with excitement, I threw all 26 racks on the bed and told Diamond to come out her clothes. With no reluctance she obeyed and we had passionate sex for about an hour, the when we were through, hundreds, twenty's and fifties were stuck all over her ass, back, thighs, and breast. I returned a few calls before we both hopped in the shower, then I put her up on our scheme.

2
Mercedes

"So tell me young lady, what brings you here to my establishment?" He asked in a controlled and calculated tone.

Gustavo "Gus" Rodriguez was my dad's longtime supplier. He had half the law enforcement on the east coast under his influence. I remembered seeing him at most of dad's "business" parties but I hadn't put two and two together until about a year before dad died.

"I need a plug" I answered, speaking with authority and doing my best to disguise how nervous I was.

"You need a what young lady?" he responded with just a hint of surprise.

"A connect Mr. Rodriguez", I said with sheer determination. "Look, I know what you and my daddy had going on. Even though he never told me, my eyes are open too. I'm not here on the strength of his reputation and I ain't looking for no favors. You can act like you don't know what I'm talking about or you can do what you been doing since day one and take a chance with me too!"

When he smiled, I knew I had him but I kept my game face on.

"Sometimes in this life big balls will get you killed, you know that right?" He asked. "But for some strange reason I don't feel offended by you coming into my place of business with demands. I do however have a demand for you." He said.

"What's your demand?" I asked with curiosity.

"Get naked." He said.

I looked in his eyes and that warm, friendly presence was replaced with a cold, deadly seriousness. It never crossed my mind that I would have to give him some pussy to get what I needed.

I stood up and took off everything until I was butt ass naked. He too stood and examined me closely, "Answer your phone in exactly 48 hours" he said and then walked out the room leaving me naked, cold, and confused.

I didn't realize what Gus did until later when I made it back to the hood, guess I passed that test! I was willing to do almost anything even give up some pussy; we were desperately in need of a plug. As soon as I got out of the car, my phone rang it was Alexus.

"Hello?" I answered.

"Where you at?" she asked.

"Just pulling up to the crib. Why what's up?"

"We need to do something about them Str8Drop niggas she said sounding irritated. "And let the streets know that Queens Up ain't for the bullshit!"

"What I tell you about talking on my line like that? Meet me in Lincoln Field Projects in about an hour. I gotta handle something real quick. Bring Jordan with you", I told her.

"Yeah hoe!" she said and hung up in my face.

"Rude bitch!" I said out loud to myself. After hanging up with Lexus I called the apartment owner for this spot I had been looking at on 171st street and 104th Ave in Perrine. It's perfect for a trap even though we may have a few run-ins with these niggas about opening up shop in their hood. But we'll cross that bridge when we get to it.

I met up with the owner for the duplex, signed all the necessary forms and paid the first and last months' rent then took off on my way to the Lincoln Field Projects to meet up with Alexus and see what got her tampon bloody. We rented a studio apartment on the back side of the projects to make a couple moves and build up some clientele. When I pulled in the parking lot Jordan was just getting out of his 2016 Nissan Maxima.

"Hey bitch!" He yelled when our eyes met.

"What's up J-Dubb?" I shot back. J-Dubb is a name that Alexus made stick to Jordan and we all called him by it.

"We about to see, Alexus and Kenya's cars are parked in their normal spots so they must be inside waiting on us," he said. We both made our way to the apartment I used my key to open the door Alexus and Kenya were both on the couch watching TV.

"Hey J-Dubb! Hey Mercedes!" They simultaneously greeted us. The TV was tuned onto the local news but the volume was barely audible.

"Now what was you talkin about on my line earlier?" I asked Alexus.

"Like I was saying, we need to finish this beef with these Str8Drop niggas because we all know it's not over. Y'all killed one of them and sent two more to the intensive care unit." She said "and just because they ain't retaliated yet doesn't mean they just gon' let that shit ride!"

"She's right!" Kenya said. "Plus it's only four of us and who knows how many of them."

"Who the fuck is the head of they squad?" Jordan asked.

"Some nigga named Peanut, but he stay confined deep in the shadows. The only time you can maybe run down on him is if they rent a club and have a showcase for their record label. Why what's on ya mind? Kenya asked.

"We need this nigga Peanut then! Kill the head and the body dead! Fuck goin back and forth with his goons! We get Peanut and a couple top niggas and everybody else just goin bow down," Jordan said.

"How we gon' do that if he don't show his face?" Kenya asked.

"I think we can pull it off, but only through patience so let's just keep our eyes opened and our ears glued to the streets," I told them. "And oh! I think I found us a plug!"

"Good, bout time! I been dry for too long.," Jordan said.

"Plus I finalized a six month lease for this duplex in Perrine that we goin' trap out of" I told them. "So Kenya I need you to start putting you face on the scene around there because it's goin be yours to manage.'

"Alright, I'm gon' get on that ASAP. You got the keys?" She asked.

"I'm gon' get them to you by tomorrow. Just chill and Jordan, I prefer you to be bustin plays off the phone because we need you to be mobile.'

"That's real" J-Dubb responded. "I already got a few customers on standby."
"You know what I was thinkin'?" Alexus asked.

"What?" We all asked simultaneously.

"We can make this a trap too." She said.

I thought about it for a second. "We need a few more soldiers. Kenya what's up with Neno?" You think he ready for this life?"

"I'm gon' slide up on him and get in his chest." She told me.

"Alright well everybody put y'all plays in motion case this shit just got real! Oh and look these spots ain't gon' look like no traps either. They goin' to look like ordinary cribs. No pleasure, straight business." Alexus said. "Is my Queens Up?" She asked. "Well let's make it shake."

3

Jordan

After I parted ways with my Queens, I bent a couple corners and ended up at the Dolphin store on 46th street and 34th Ave in Brown Subs. It's only called the "Dolphin Store" because it has the Miami Dolphins logo painted on it, but it's really just the 24-hour convenience store. You can get chips, cookies, crack, heroine, weed, pills, condoms, and cash off your food stamp all at the same damn time.

I went to let a few niggas know that I was back on deck and the drought was finally over. As I pulled up I saw my nigga Torch comin out of the store with a pack of Newports and a Red Bull in one hand while holdin up his pants with the other. "Damn. What dey do Torch?" I asked while still posted in the car.

"Who dat?' He asked while cluctchin his pistol revealin the handle of the chrome gun he had on his waist.

"This J-Dubb nigga!"

"Oh shit, bruh you 'round here wit' the bullshit! You was about to get yo ass painted red! Damn, where you been at?"

"Shit, I been coolin' it. Trying to connect some dots you know? Trying to build me a stairway to heaven since they say that the sky is the limit."

"I hear that chicken talk, fly shit you spittin but it's crazy how you pop up right after some niggas just slid through here lookin for you".

"What niggas!?" I asked instantly on alert and checking my surroundings.

"Them Str8Drop niggas!"

"Oh yeah? What they was lurkin in?"

"An all-black Ford Explorer, an older model with some dark ass tints and a paper tag."

"How many niggas Torch?"

"Shit they was in a new Ford Five Hundred too, it was silver. It looked like a rental, they was at least 8 niggas deep but I told them you don't be around here no more."

"What else you told them?"

"Come on J-Dubb stop sizing my shit! What the fuck I look like? I don't rock like that!" he said.

"My bad, I'm just checkin."

"You ain't gotta check me. I'm solid and I fucks wit you. You need to fuck with me, let me eat off the plate wit you!"

"Yeah you right and I'm wit you when you right. I tell you what, the next time any of them niggas come through here tell them that you can set me up for the right price. Then lead them to me. I'll put you all the way on and let you make yo own plate". I reached in my secret stash spot under the steering wheel and took out some work I had on me and passed him one of the sandwich bags. "Here go half a zip, 14 grams of the purest cocaine in south Florida. You can rock it up or keep it soft, whatever; just don't step on it!" I told him. "That's on me. Next one on you."

"Good lookin." He said as I reversed out of the parking lot and eased off.

I made a right on 27th Avenue goin north, on my way to Opa-Locka when I spotted a sliver Ford Five Hundred slidin' through the white tops housing projects. I followed it at a safe distance. They stopped at the BP gas station on MLK Street and 22nd Ave, across the street from the Cultural Arts Center in Liberty City. I parked across the street and watched but they didn't seem to be paying attention, it was two niggas with dreads inside the car. After pumping gas they pulled off but I was still on the trail.

They drove east on MLK Street and made a left turn onto the infamous 18th Ave, notoriously known for drugs, prostitution and an extremely high body count. I followed them to 67th Street where the Ford Five Hundred stopped at the corner house and parked. Guess what I saw in the yard? A black 2001 Ford Explorer with Limo tinted windows! I kept it pushing though, the time on the dashboard of my 2016 Nissan Maxima read 12:45 am

I slid to my lil' duck off in Hialeah that even my Queens didn't know about. I quickly put on my special purpose lace wig, changed from my Levi's and Timberland boots to a hot pink flower patterned sun dress. I put on my special made butt pads and padded bra with a light coat of makeup including some lip gloss. Hell I even put some fake eyes on. When I was finished I looked like Wendy Williams up close and K. Michelle from a distance. I took my Chinese version of the M-16 from the shelf in the closet and placed it into my oversized hot pink Chanel bag.

    I drove a couple blocks away to the Hialeah Hospital where I kept my burgundy 2003 Ford Taurus I the parking garage. I switched cars, putting my bag in the trunk, then headed back to 67th street, NW 18th Ave. An entire hour had passed before I made it back but both the Ford Five Hundred and the Ford Explorer were exactly where I last saw them.

    Five niggas and two females were standing in the yard, leaning on the Explorer listening to music. I parked next door and killed the engine. I then turned the interior light on just long enough for them to see my lace wig as I pretended to look in the mirror, fixing my makeup. I scrolled through my phone for about a good 30 seconds trying to give the impression that I was waiting on somebody. It worked too because they didn't pay me much attention.

I opened my door and proceeded to exit my whip. I walked around the front of the car pretending to check my front passenger tire for damage, and immediately I felt all eyes take notice. I pretended not to hear the whistles and using my alarm pad, I popped the trunk. Slowly, seductively and provocatively swayed to the now opened trunk. I felt all eyes on glued to my coke bottle, apple bottom. I bent over into the trunk making it my business to advertise my voluptuous and curvaceous ass.

"Excuse me sexy." I heard one of them say. But by this time, I had my M-16 held firmly with two hands. I turned around real cool but swift like.

"Who me?" I asked squeezing the trigger killing him and 3 more of them instantly. Glass shattered as the bullets hit the Explorer and chewed through the metal. The other 3 took off running in different directions but even the road runner couldn't out run a bullet

The gun range paid off as I aimed, hitting the bitch who took off running, right in the center of her back. Last but not least, I braced myself as I aimed to terminate the last of the group.

I fired once to the left making him flinch to the right and then I fired twice hitting him in the back of the head and neck. Before his lifeless body crashed to the pavement I was running back to the car and quickly but carefully tore through the night.

4

Kenya

Perrine is the hood for real! It can't get too much more savage than this. It's a trap on damn near every street, plus you had niggas posted on corners short stopping every change they could.

I was just slidin through checking out the scene trying to see what type of competition I was up against.

Alexus had given me five grand to deck out the spot. I know that she knew five racks was not going to cover everything but I somehow made it work.

I purchased two full bedroom sets from Rent-A-Center, spent 15 hundred on a nice ass living room set from Badcock Furniture and bought two 57 inch

Plasma TV's from Wal-Mart for almost 18 hundred. With the last thousand dollars, I bought pots, pans, dishes, utensils, rugs, a bathroom set and everything else that would turn a house into a home. I even spent some of my own money on a fish tank and some lil ugly ass gold fish.

On my way back from Wal-mart I rode through the Circle Plaza Projects in Perrine. There was a group of niggas in a circle shooting dice. I stopped and rolled down my window.

"Who got some high grade round here?" I asked drawing the attention of every nigga at the dice game.

"What?" One of them responded.

"Who got some dro' or some kush round here? I asked again.

"We don't fuck wit the police" somebody said.

"What?!" I asked throwing my car into park and hopping out in the middle of the street.

"Who the fuck said that?" I asked, walking towards the group.

"Me! Who the fuck you think you is?!" some short dark skinned dude with deep waves and a mouth full of gold teeth said.

"Listen fuck nigga, I don't know who you think you is but let that be the last time yo' pussy ass disrespect me, ol' broke, lil dick ass nigga! I'll run yo bitch ass off this block!" I said while reaching in my purse and coming out with my .380 already cocked and one in the head. "You got the wrong bitch!" I said with the gun pointed at the ground but damn sure ready for use.

"Calm down lil mama!" one of the dudes said to me, walking towards me with his hands up, "Calm down, calm down please! Put that gun away and sit in the car, we don't need no problems! We just bein' careful out here we ain't never saw you round here before. I ain't got no dro or no Kush but I got some sour diesel just please calm down."

"You betta check that nigga," I said keeping my eyes on all of them and back pedaling to my car gun still in hand.

"I only got six dimes on me how much you need?" he asked.

"Let me get all six of them" I said reaching into my bra with my free hand and pulling out a single hundred dollar bill. "Give that bum ass nigga the change!" I said hopping in my 2012 Nissan Altima and pulling off. It's a small world so I know I'm going to run into that fuck boy again, so I made a mental note to stay alert and I called my cousin Neno just in case. I may need him to put in some work.

"What's good Kenya?" he answered

"Shit chillin' at my new lil spot in Perrine, where you at?"

"I'm on Gould's Park watchin' these niggas play football" he said.

"Can you get away for a lil bit?" I asked.

"Come on Kenya why you askin' me that dumb ass question? You know I only answer to God and money. You only call when it's bout some money so you comin' to get me or what?"

"Boy get off my line, I'll be there in about twenty minutes." I said while shaking my head to his response.

Neno is my big cousin he's only older than me by a month and two days but the way he makes it seem you would swear he's twenty years older. We both turned 26 just a few months ago.

Neno been tugging' ever since I could remember; he has been locked up in some kind of corrections facility more than he has been free! From juvenile to prison, he always had my back and to me his loyalty was unquestionable. He just got out of prison after doing a 3 year bid for possession of a fire arm by convicted felon and I know he's trying to get on his feet.

Eventually I picked him up from the park and brought him back to the spot in Perrine. I explained to him the movement that Queens Up has going on. I let him know the role that we needed him to play and I also filled him in on the beef we had with them Str8Drop niggas. He listened quietly as I layed everything out for him and only spoke when I was apparently finished speaking.

"Kenya I just got out the pen and I ain't got a pot to piss in! I'm ready to get this money!" Was all he said.

5

Diamond

"Shawty I don't mind if you dance on that pole, that don't make you a hoe. Shawty I don't mind if you work until 3, long as you leaving wit me. Gon' get yo money, money money, Yo Money, money, money."

Usher Raymond blaring through the industrial sound system had these hoes turned up! It was raining money and believe me when I tell you; them hoes didn't mind getting wet!

Tonight was the grand opening at the Club Free Money and given the fact that the line was wrapped around the parking lot, I would say that the owner did a pretty good job at promoting. For the past couple weeks, club Free Money was being talked about all over Facebook. Everybody that was anybody was making sure that they had their face in the place tonight.

It looked like the B.E.T awards up in here, niggas was dressed to impress and these bitches were barely dressed! The parking lot had to be worth more than a couple million with all the foreign cars in it, from Maseratis to Bentleys, Range Rovers and the latest Benzes. This use to be Club Coco's until Free Money Ent. bought and remolded it.

Club Free Money has two floors, the ground floor was constructed with red-brick tiles, giving it an 1930s antique look; once actually stepping foot inside you immediately felt the presence of money. The main floor of the club is the size of a football field and the bar is positioned on what would be the fifty yard line. The bartenders have their own personal flight of stairs that takes them from the bar downstairs to the bar up in the glass house. 82 inch plasmas were evenly and strategically spaced out; mounted on the walls of the first floor. There are pool tables and another section with tables and private booths on the outlying the dance floor.

Though there were several different hoods in the club, the atmosphere wasn't hostile. Everybody was dancing, sipping, smoking, throwing money and just hanging the fuck out! Most clubs I've been to in the urban communities always had drama and tension, but tonight it seemed that all the hood beefs and cat fights were put to aside and everybody was on "stunt mode".

The club is so huge that I hadn't checked out the second floor until an hour after I got inside. When I made it to the top of the stairs, it seemed like I was in an entirely different club. The walls were made of glass and I could see out into the parking lot still filled with people eager to get in. The interior walls were also glass and none of the private booths were really private, they had different color tints on them that could still be seen through.

There were three stripper poles within ten feet of each other on a glass stage and the strippers were competing for money that was being thrown. Off to the side of the club were the VIP booths, they all had personal strip poles, and smaller glass stages. In the general VIP section there were several tables furnished with buckets of ice, crystal glasses and bottles of Jay-Z's "Ace of Spades" champagne. The VIP section alone cost three hundred dollars per person.

Celebrities could be found in the VIP section, which had its own entrance and exit to an underground parking garage. Trick Daddy, Plies, Young Jeezy, BG, Remy Ma, Dwane Wade, and Floyd Mayweather were just a few I had managed to see so far. You had everything from hoodstars to trapstars and even porn stars all eager to flaunt their riches.

Everybody was reppin' their hoods, St8Drop was definitely in the building changing these hoes financial situations. They savage life niggas from the neighborhood known as Narania were also in the building along with G-Rated, Queens Up, Gunline, and a whole bunch of other cliques. It seemed like everywhere I turned niggas was walking around with "sex, money, murder" chains on studded with rubies and diamonds. I came to the club alone, while Zetta was in the streets handling business as usual. Don't get it twisted! I came to the club to enjoy myself but I was looking for my next victim at the same time.

I paid the 300 dollars and made my way through the VIP section, turning heads as I seductively swayed to the music. I decided to post up at the one of the tables because going into a booth would hide all the ass I'm carrying on my five foot seven, 140 pound frame.

I went to the Aventura mall yesterday to get something to wear specifically for this event. I was decked out in a 2 piece spandex Dolce and Gabbana bodysuit. It was burgundy and graciously complimented my golden brown complexion and matched perfectly with the burgundy streaks in my blonde hair. The stretchy material clung to every curve of my body and exposed every dimple in my ass. I set it off with some three inch gold Jimmy Choo pumps and some simple gold accessories. I got my finger and toe nails polished clear with a thin gold strip at the tips. I am the definition of a "Jazzy Bitch". I been in the club now for about two hours and I have yet to see a bitch that could come close to the natural beauty that I possessed. I'm just a Diamond in the ruff.

As I grind to the music and sipped on my cup of Nuvo a bartender and two strippers approached my table. "Excuse me miss" the bartender says.

"Yes, how may I help you?" I asked a bit confused.

"These two ladies were hired to keep you company and this", he said pulling a bottle of champagne from a bucket of ice," is our most expensive spirit, it's called Monte de Blanco priced at 32 hundred a bottle. It was sent also, just in case you got thirsty" Before I got a chance to thank him, Rich Homie Quan stepped in and handed the bartender a healthy bundle of miscellaneous bills.

"I got it from here, thank you," he said to the bartender who put the bottle and glasses on the table, turned around and disappeared into the crowd on the dance floor. The two strippers just stood there and vibed to the music, exchanging words between each other.

"How you doing sexy?" he asked, with too much confidence.

"Fine and yourself?" I replied, not exhibiting signs of being no groupie.

"Do you always go to clubs by yourself?"

"I don't need company to enjoy myself" I replied.

"I can feel that, but I sent these females over her to keep you company. I paid them good too but I'mma tell them to bust off."

"Nah, they good but I could've paid them whatever it is that you paid them myself."

"Is that true? Damn, what I paid them for a couple hours most people don't make in a month!" he said obviously bragging.

"Well I'm glad that I'm not most people and if you don't mind, I would really like to get back to enjoying myself." I said politely dismissing him.

"Are you serious?" he asked completely shocked.

"As a heart attack." I leaned over and whispered in his ear.

He turned around and disappeared just as quickly as he had appeared. I know he felt some type of way. Rich Homie Quan has money, but he also has too much attention at the moment. I'm about business, my pleasure is in the streets taking penitentiary chances to make sure I can afford Gucci and Louis Vuitton.

Zetta is my down ass bitch and it's crazy because two years ago, I had no thoughts about being with another woman. She has proved herself plenty of times and ain't nothing coming between what we got going on. Most people use L.O.L for "laugh out loud" but to me it means "Loyalty over life" and I plan on remaining loyal to Zetta until death do us apart.

I pulled a thousand dollars from my wallet and asked the bouncer to get me straight ones. He came back about 5 minutes later with ten stacks of dollar bills in a bread basket. I took a stack removed the money band and slung it in the air over the two strippers that were still standing near my table. When they saw the money rain down they turned around and came closer to where I was. One of them pulled the chair out from the table and the other one gently pushed me in it. They both took turns dancing in front of me. Everybody in the VIP section had their eyes on us and we put on a pretty interesting show.

After we calmed down and was back to just vibing to the music and sipping the Monte de Blanco compliments of Rich Homie, a female bartender approached me. "Excuse me, I don't mean to bother you but I got paid to tell you that one of our guest would like to have a word with you." She said, while smiling and counting a small stack of money.

"Okay well go back and ask your guest why did he or she send you?" I said, doing my best to be polite. I trailed her with my eyes to see if she would expose who her guest. She strutted to a VIP booth where about five strippers and three guys were posted. They had bottles of Hennessy, Remy, and Grey Goose decorating their table. I could tell their ranks because two of them were hands on interacting with the strippers the third one just leaned back calm, cool and collected.

He's the boss! He was sipping straight from a bottle of Monte de Blanco and from about 30 feet away I could see that he didn't have a chain on like his goons. He sported a three finger connector ring that had the letters "S.M.M" flooded with red diamonds.

His eyes were fixed on me as he ignored what was taking place inside his booth. The female bartender leaned over and whispered in his ear, but he didn't open his mouth to respond, just nodded his head. I could tell he was a big fish and I had to bait him up good. Finally he stood, said a few words to his entourage then smoothly swagged over to my table.

"I do apologize for sendin' the message instead of deliverin' it myself." He said in an authorative but controlled voice.

"Yeah, you see it got returned to sender." I replied being friendly and inviting. I had to give him props though, he was dripping ice from his ears, wrist and hands. This nigga even had rubies in his mouth. He was decked in Gucci from his shoes to his hat and I was willing to bet my last dime that his boxers and tank top were Gucci too.

"My name is Gucci by the way and I would definitely love to become acquainted with you," he said with pure confidence.

A gangster with a brain huh? I made a mental note to be extra cautious. No room for error. Lights, camera, action! "Nice to meet you Mr. Gucci, my name is Sania and I wouldn't mind having a friendly conversation," I said putting a strong emphasis on friendly.

"Well do you mind if we go into a separate booth to just sit and talk?" he asked.

"Actually I would not mind that at all, this Monte de Blanco is sneaking up on me," I lied.

I briefly exchanged small talk with the two strippers as we exchanged numbers because me and Zetta had just installed a strip pole at home that we needed tested. Then me and Gucci made our way to the private booth. In the booth next to ours sat Kevin Gates, Future and a couple more important looking people. They all spoke to Gucci and that made me wonder. Did I catch a fish or do I have a great White Shark on my line?

We held a pretty decent conversation which surprised me. Gucci seemed educated, sophisticated and extremely calculated. We talked for an hour nonstop before being interrupted by his goons.

"Big homie you straight?" they asked, checking the surroundings.

"Yeah y'all just play the shadows." He said. "Now where were we?" he asked, giving me his undivided attention.

"Well to tell you the truth, it's gettin' late and I gotta be to work in a couple of hours so I really should be headin' home," i said.

"Where do you work?" He asked. But I was in control of this conversation and two steps ahead of him.

"I'm a paralegal for an industrial law firm." I lied.

"Damn! I should've been a paralegal if they paying enough to buy a 32 hundred dollar bottle of champagne. A 300 dollar VIP ticket and be decked out in Dolce and Gabbana," he said. "I thought you were a model."

Blushing, I said, "Do you mind walking me to my car?"

"I don't mind at all," he said doing a hand signal to his goons who were in the middle of lap dances. They immediately stood to attention and became extra alert. As we exited the club his goons escorted us. One walked about ten feet ahead and the other about five feet behind.

"Do you always have personal security?" I asked.

"No not always but I must stay on point and plus they my nephews".

I led the way to my car and when we got there Gucci said, "A 2014 Mercedes Benz CLK55 Limited Edition! That's a nice vehicle for an even nicer lady."

I blushed again, not trying to seem eager for his compliments; we exchanged phone numbers and made plans for a more formal outing together.

The great white shark has taken the bait. Now all I have to do is reel him in.

6

Mercedes

"First thing first, let's get this straight. I never really liked your father. So me dealin' with you has absolutely nothin' to do with him", he started. "What I saw in him, I don't see in you." I sat there quietly listening.

"I'm a very well respected powerful man, which I'm sure you already know. Your money is no good with me this time, next time I collect every penny! Inside your trunk there's a bag with a key of the purest cocaine you're gonna find in South Florida. Do as you please with it." He said.

He didn't ask for me to speak and I didn't volunteer a response. Through my experiences I was aware that actions spoke volumes where words were nothing more than an attempt to be heard. He stood from his seat and I followed suit, we shook hands symbolizing a contract then one of his guards escorted me to my BMW. I pulled out of the thick iron gates with mixed emotions.

Why would Gus give me a whole key for free? Especially when I was prepared to pay for it? How the fuck did he get in my car? What else did he put in here? I searched under my passenger's seat and my Tek9 was still there.

Gus lived in a very secluded neighborhood and it took about 15 minutes just to make it to the nearest interstate. Another 20 minutes south on I-95 and I was forced to get off at the Liberty City exit because my gas light had come on.

About four blocks away from the highway exit a silver 2013 Ford Taurus pulled out behind me. I cautiously turned the corner and it turned with me. I tried to look in my rear view mirror but the tinted windshield of the Taurus made it impossible to see through. I bent another corner and it followed. The sun had just set and i weighed my options. I went to reach for my Tek9 that's when I heard the siren and saw the flashing blue and red lights. As soon as I contemplated making a run for it, a gold Dodge Ram 1500 pulled I front of me blocking my path. All the doors of the Dodge flew open and two officers emerged from the Taurus with guns drawn, yelling demands.

"Damn!" I followed directions turning my car off and putting my hands out the window. Two detectives approached my car, one on the driver's side and his partner on the other.

"License and registration," he said while his partner shined his flashlight through the interior of my car.

"It smells like marijuana in your car, have you been smoking? He asked, shining his light in my eyes and reaching for my permits. They didn't even bother to run my license or anything, which made me more afraid than I already was.

"I need you to step out of the car nice and slow." He said.

"For what? Y'all haven't even ran my license."

"Hey! Don't you fucking back talk me! Get your ass out of the car now before I shoot you for disobeying an officer!" he screamed furiously with his hand on his service pistol.

I slowly opened the door and got out with my hands in the air. The detectives handcuffed me immediately and patted me down. They were all dressed in black, the only color coming from their Miami Gardens Police Department logos stitched on their bullet proof vests. I had just left Gus house in Miami Gardens and they were about 30 miles out of their jurisdiction so I knew this was serious business.

Damn! I was placed in the back of the Ford Taurus and some strange shit happened next, the four detectives got back in the Dodge Ram, one got in my BMW and the other got in the Ford Taurus and drove one behind the other to the Miami Gardens Police Department!

Investigation Room
9:48 PM

They put me in the interrogation room over an hour ago and it's cold as fuck. Damn, how I let this happen? Just as I get ready to put my head down the door opened, the two detectives who drove the Ford Taurus walk in.

"Choose your answers wisely" the shorter detective warns before they both sit down across from me.

I don't respond.

"Where were you coming from when we stopped you?" his partner asks.

"I just came from the swap shop in Ft. Lauderdale why?" I ask with an attitude.

"I ask the questions!" he screams, slamming his fists on the table. I roll my eyes at him, doing my best to mask the fear that's threatening overtake me.

"Where did you detour after you left Ft. Lauderdale?"

"I didn't detour nowhere!"

"So where did you get that key of cocaine from in your trunk? And that Tek9 under the front passenger seat?" he asks in an aggravated tone.

"First off, I don't own no fucking cocaine and I have never even saw a Tek9 in my life!" I lie in an equally aggravated tone.

The partner who up until this point remained quiet, stood and screamed, "Listen you little tramp, we know who you got that cocaine from and we followed you from his house."

Then he pulled his cell phone out and showing me pictures of my car leaving Gus' house. "Now yo have two options," he says. "One you can keep playing games like were some stupid fucking rookies or you can help us help you".

It's death before dishonor with me because as far as I'm concerned dishonor is punishable by death and death only so..."Look detectives" I say, with an attitude "I don't know shit about no cocaine! For all I know y'all could've put it in there. And if I did I would never work for no pigs! Now if I'm being charged with something please let's get it over with.

Immediately the door opens and in comes the chief dressed impressively in a Tom Ford tailor made suit.

"Good" he says and throwing me my phone and keys. "Now get the fuck out of my station and I never want to see you again." Then he disappears quickly as he had appeared.

"What?" was all I could say.

"Your car is parked outside, here is your license and registration. The exits is that way!" the loud detective says pointing to the exit sign.

They didn't have to repeat it again. I damn near ran up out that shit.

Inside my car the Tek 9 was exactly back under the seat. "I'll check that later!" I was determined to get as far away from the Police Station AQAP (as quick as possible). I drove straight to Perrine after first stopping at the gas station.

After a 45 minute drive, I cut the car off and hopped out in front of the duplex. My phone went of scaring the shit out of me in the process. It was Alexus.

"Hoe, what's up?" I answered the call.

"Bitch you betta watch yo mouth!" she said, "I can be a bitch all day, but if you call me one more hoe I'mma see if yo' hands up to date. And where the hell you at? J-Dubb said he been tryna to call you!

"Bitch ass hoe, I just got to the spot. But Kenya ain't here. So I'm finna go in and handle some shit, I'mma call you back in about 30 minutes".

"Yeah hoe Bye!" she said hanging up in my face. My sister Alexus is my best friend and we been through the toughest situations together. I popped the trunk, got out and checked my surroundings because like I said before, Perrine is the hood and the Police be patrolling on the regular, not to mention the snitches, haters and the jack boys.

When I looked in the trunk I couldn't believe my eyes, the bag was still there but instead of one brick it was two! With the bag in hand, I casually and cautiously made my way inside the duplex. I had to give Kenya her credit, she had furnished the place just the way I wanted it. After settling in I called J-Dubb and Kenya asking to break the bricks down into ounces. 72 to be exact.

I called Alexus back and filled her on everything that had taken place and I assured her that I would take care of the crew until she returned from out of town in three days. As soon as, I hung up the phone I heard keys opening the front door. I grabbed my Tek 9 and hit the lights. In walks J-Dubb I flipped on the lights. After seeing that everything was kosher I put the gun down and blew the breath I was holding.

Jordan started smiling and Kenya had Neno with her.

"What's up" Neno greeted me looking

"Whats's good hoe?" J- Dubb said, "Damn you get straight to work huh?" While looking at all the ounces and scales I had laid across the dining room table.

"Yep" I said answering J-Dubbs question and the directing my attention to Kenya. "Good job with the decorations, did you check out the neighborhood?"

"Yeah" she said, "I had to snap on some nigga but it looks like it's some kind of drug being sold on every corner!"

"Okay Kenya we don't need no more drama right, now so chill yo' lil ass down." I replied shaking my head though I liked that no nonsense gangster shit she was on.

"Where you get this from?" Jordan asked, picking up one of the ounces. "It smells like fingernail polish remover and looks like fish scales."

"Let me see", Neno anxiously asked, grabbing the sandwich bag from Jordan.

Kenya went in the kitchen and pulled out a pink glass beaker and some baking soda. "I'm about to drop one of see how much I can bring back". Kenya was a beast when it came to bringing 28 grams of coke back to 42 grams of rock hard crack-cocaine. "Call old school Eddie and tell him to come through and test this shit out and spread the word", Kenya told J-Dubb.

"No!" I said. "We don't need him telling nobody shit! The only thing that get sold from here is half ounces or better. No nickel or dimin', I suggest you make sure you know who you're dealing with because every nigga and his momma confidential informants.

"Yeaa you right" Kenya affirmed.

"Some crazy shit happened to me today that bowed my mind but I ain't gon' sneak on it just yet. That's why I'm telling y'all in so many words to keep y'all eyes up and stay on point!" I said seriously.

"What's understood ain't gotta be explained", Neno said.

Somebody knocked on the door. Jordan was the first to pull his P90 rugger out. Kenya grabbed her .380 from out of nowhere as I was taking my gun off safety. Neno's eyes were big as hell. Kenya was already in the kitchen shutting off the circuit breakers. It was pitch black now, the only light coming from the street lamps casting its glow through the cracks. "It's me" I heard a female voice say.

"That's Alexus!" Jordan confirmed.

"Open the door, I'mma beat this hoe ass! I said turning the lights back on as Jordan opened the door and there stood Alexus with a huge smirk on her face.

"Hoe you always playing, you almost got that blond wig dyed red." I said with an attitude.

"I had to see what kind of security y'all had" she said, unable to stop laughing.

"You told me you was still in Tamps!" I said to her.

"Bitch this ain't the first time, I lied to and it won't be the last!" She said, while checking out the spot. "You did yo' thank up in here Kenya," she added.

"Did you see the 11'oclock news? Some female killed like 4 or 5 of them Str8drop niggas and two hoes! Neno said.

"That's 7 we don't have to worry about then", Kenya commented.

"It was me" Jordan revealed with a blank expression as if killing was equivalent to passing gas or something.

What?!" we all asked simultaneously!

"Y'all heard me don't act like y'all don't know that really bout that life!" he said clearly feeling himself.

How?" I asked shaking my head in disbelief.

"Mercedes it don't matter, the problem needed handling so I handled it. Like some shit straight out of a movie. He said, laughing. "I'll wish I knew where that nigga Peanut was at I'll run down on that shit too!'

"Calm down" I said to J-Dubb "and where the fuck you been at? I asked Alexus, still feeling some type of way about her lying.

"At the castle going over the paperwork" She shot back.

"The castle?" asked Kenya. "What's the castle?"

"Home" Alexus answered. We haven't been to the castle since our dad was killed a year and a half ago, it was our dad's biggest house and he left it to our mom who hasn't stepped foot in there since. If Alexus was there then that means that she's been doing some research to find out who killed out dad.

"Did you come up anything?" I inquired.

"I was checkin'", she paused and then pulled me out of ear-range of the clique. "I was checking out the surveillance cameras and the footage from around the time dad got killed"

"And?"

"And daddy was there a lot more than usual during those last couple of days he was alive, we need to go over it again together in case I missed something," she said.

"Alright but it's almost three o'clock in the mornin' so let's get this over with," I said referring to the ounces that were on the table.

Me and Alexus distributed the work and gave everybody a post. Jordan gave Neno his .45 from under the seat of his Maxima. We made plans to get Neno a car and he would stay at the spot to work it off a little at time. Then I let them all know what I expected it to take; we all went our separate ways. Leaving Neno at the spot in Perrine.

7

Zetta

"What's up LJ?" I said answering my phone.

"I'm almost there" he said.

"Alright, pull in the back." I told him

LJ is one of my custos, he be doing his thing and I been trying to really put him on. He was still a lil young, just turning 20 but I see loyalty in him from a mile away. If I was out of the area he wouldn't just run to the next supplier like most hustlers, he would sit patiently and wait on me. I always threw him a lil extra cushion and I know that played a role too, but with a lil guidance he could be trusted to be my outlet.

"I'll be right back bae," I told Diamond leaving her at the salon in the flea market. She ain't even question me and I didn't have to, she was my other half and knew every move I made and vice versa.

U.S.A Flea Market on 79th street and 30th avenue is a one stop shop. Everybody, they mama and their grandma be up in this bitch. Both the front and back parking lots were packed with everything from BMWs to old ass station wagons. Some people were outside posted by their cars vibin. Cars were lined up at the music shop waiting to get their speakers hooked up.

I went to my Daytona 500 Special Edition Dodge Challenger, (Thanks to Dread) and cut the AC on. I lit the joint that I had left in the ash tray. My phone vibrated. It was LJ, but I had already saw his 2006 Chevy Monte Carlo on 24's turning into the parking lot. I answered "I'm looking at yo' car, come to the last row" I said while getting out the car.

When LJ saw me he stopped behind my car turning his hazard lights on. "Damn Zetta when you got that?" he asked, pointing at my car.

"It's a rental." I lied.

"You gone let me hold it?" he asked excitedly.

"Boy, we'll talk about that later, here get this" I said giving him a pound of Dreads Mango Kush inside of a Coach Book bag. "Call me when you got my money, I gotta go Diamond inside waitin' on me". As soon as I said that Diamond, was walking outside.

"You in trouble" LJ said playfully.

"Bae why you ain't answerin the phone?" she asked "What's up LJ?" she said then turned back to me waiting on an answer.

I checked my pockets, "It's in the car," I said.

"Oh you had me worried because you wasn't pickin up" she said.

"Nah, I'm good bae. I'm finna finish smoking my joint in the ash tray and I'mma be in there. Go get yo hair done. I ain't tryna be up here all day" I told her and without a word she turned around and walked back inside.

"I'm finna go bust a few plays. I'mma hit you up later," LJ said.

"True, just fuck wit me" I said as he pulled off.

I got back in the car and fired my joint back up. I sat there allowing my thoughts to run free. I was thinking about how I got to this point in my life. I was 14 years old when I met Keon, he was about 19 or 20. Keon was naturally in shape at about five feet eleven, 160 pounds. He was light brown with neatly twisted dreads. He had a six inch permanent scar on his face from a fight he had in jail (I think). Some people might say that the scar was his only physical flaw but to me it added character. He had the most defined hazel brown eyes and a mouth full of gold. I hadn't had dick since I met Diamond but just thinkin about him had my pussy wet.

I use to be fucked up about Keon but I wasn't no groupie like them other hoes that ran behind him. I had just jumped off the porch, learnin' fraudulent schemes when I met him. He used to be on my trail heavy back then but I just gave him the cold shoulder.

By the time I was 16 I was already a vet with the fraud game and to be a teenager I was running circles around bitches in the hood. All it took was one time for me to get robbed before I got me a lil chrome .25 caliber pistol. One day while at the park I had got into it with some envious ass holes and they jumped me. I had my pistol in my Dooney and Burke handbag and when I broke free from them hoes I pulled it out and shot at them.

Keon was at the park too, he was the reason I was able to break free. He did everything accept punch one of them hoes in they shit. Then he came and took the gun out of my hand. He walked me to his car and told me to stay there, he talked to one of his homeboys came back and then got me off the scene just as the police sirens were getting close.

Since then me and Keon was more like friends than anything. He never pressured me for a relationship and made me fall in love with him. About 5 months later we were officially a couple. Throughout our year and a half relationship, I learned so much about life in general from that nigga.

That's when I found out how blind "love" really is. Keon was a natural born hustla and he had a lil respect in the streets but he wasn't bout shit because he couldn't stop cheating, it got so bad that he didn't even try to hide it no more. The final straw was when he started putting his hands on me. I mean I dealt with the cheating because he brainwashed me with that "ride or die" bullshit and I was raised a loyal bitch since birth; but the beating threw a bitch for a loop. I forgave him the first time he slapped the shit out of me, blacking my eye, but my antennas went up. The second time he tried that shit, I shot his ass one time in the shoulder only because I couldn't aim for shit. I had seen my momma get her ass beat so many times that I made a promise to myself that I wouldn't be no victim and I aimed to kill that pussy nigga.

My momma couldn't stand Keon because she felt like he was the reason I had dropped out of school. I dropped out of school because school was for a better future and I needed a better present.

Keon didn't just have one hustle, he sold heroin, broke in houses and robbed. I was just into credit card fraud and Income tax schemes but he used me to set a few niggas up so he could rob them. He showed me the power that pussy had over most niggas and that was something that school would never have taught me and look at me now. I would say that I'm pretty fuckin' successful at the age of 25.

I got me a nice condo in Coral Gables, an Infiniti truck, a brand new Dodge Challenger. Nice jewelry, a closet full of top of the line clothes, safe full of money and a bad, loyal Puerto Rican bitch.

If you saw me and Diamond you wouldn't know that were gay because both of us are fem. We wear all of the top of the line designers. My shoe game sick with all my Jimmy Choos and red bottoms, same for my bitch. I'll switch it up depending on my mood, like now I got on some baggy ass True Religion jeans, some all-white 300 dollar Scotty Pippen sneakers, a white V-neck T-Shirt and a Denver Broncos snap back. Every time Diamond step out she lookin like female money. I make sure that every nigga that's eating wanna taste of her.

I hate that nigga Keon for what he put me through but I'm thankful for the experience. After my relationship with him I was 100% into women. I still had sex here or there with niggas but it was for beneficial purposes only. I ain't got no complex with fuckin for prosperity.

I stepped back inside the Flea Market until Diamond was finished getting her hair done. I got my dreads re twisted and the tips bleached. When we were finished we slid to the Olive Garden, one of Diamonds "dates" kept blowing up her phone. Some nigga named Peanut that she met at Aventura mall. He was asking could they hang out, which they had been doing a lot of lately.

In just a month she had found out about two of his stash houses. One was in Miami Lakes and the other was in North Miami Beach. Judging by what Diamond had been telling me, the nigga Peanut is high up on the food chain. I hope she right because I don't usually target workers, but if Diamond said it was worth it, then I more than trusted her judgement.

While we ate our food I called my Kush plug, I been dealing with this nigga named Devin. He got good product at reasonable prices, plus he's a pretty solid nigga. I see real written all over his character and demeanor. He's real business minded and alert. Touching him had even came across my mind, but I decided against it because Devin is in a whole other league.

I gave Diamond the green light to go chill with Peanut and start digging more into his personal life. Not too deep where he would notice and be suspicious. We finished eating, drove home and finished our conversation in the confines of our king sized pillow top mattress. After we had wrapped the business up she stripped down but ass naked and I got wet instantly.

She slowly and seductively started to undress me, her silver dollar sized nipples were erect and begging for my warm and wet tongue. I couldn't resist the temptation and I hungrily sucked on them and teased her breasts, she let out a soft moan. With my left hand I started rubbing on her swollen clit while she did the same to me. Once I was completely stripped of all my clothing, our lips locked in a passionate kiss. I lay with my eyes closed already depositing my creamy juices onto the bank of our king sized bed. When I came back from a realm that only Diamond could take me, she was standing inches away from the bed putting lubricant on our 10 inch rubber strap on.

    She aggressively shoved me on to the bed, forcing me to lay on my back, then she lay on her torso on my stomach and placed my thighs across each of her shoulders. She gently kissed my thighs and the outer edge of my pussy until I couldn't take the torture of being teased any longer I reached up, grabbed her head and rammed it into my pussy. I exploded in her mouth twice before we got into the 69 position. I did my best to penetrate her ass with my tongue, while she eagerly returned the favor.

    As I layed up under her with her perfectly round, firm ass and pretty bald pussy inches away from my face, I smiled. So many niggas would die to have tickets to this private show. I kissed both her ass cheeks then rubbed my wet tongue up and down her pussy lips, doing my best to taste her insides.

I slid two fingers inside of her warm and wet juice box, she started gyrating her hips to the rhythm of my strokes. Then I pulled my fingers out and tasted them. I locked my arm around the small of her back to bring her ass closer to my face while at the same time making sure she couldn't run.

After about 30 minutes of our oral escapade, I turned her on her stomach, and pulled her waist up to form an arch in her back. I took the bottle of lubricant and rubbed it all over the strap on, then poured the rest all over her ass and pussy. I put the strap on around my waist and slid in her nice and slow. She took it like a pro too and after just a few strokes she was throwing her pussy back in a steady motion. We changed to every position we could think of and even invented some. She must've came about 3 or 4 times and I came just watching her squirm under my pressure. I was just getting started and she was ready to tap out. I fucked her on the floor, on the bed, the shower, her ass, her mouth and her pussy until we both fell asleep.

Unfortunately, sleep didn't last long because my damn phone wouldn't stop ringing, so we both got up, took a shower and cleaned up our mess. She got ready to chill with our victim and I got fresh and hit the streets. On my way to meet Devin.

8

Alexus

I went to my mom's house in Coconut Grove because I had to know what she knew about the castle. I had a lot of questions that needed answers if I was ever going to find out who killed my dad.

"Hey, Ma", I said, walking through the door into the family room. She was sitting on the couch watching the stories. Instead of responding verbally she put a finger to her mouth telling me to be quiet and pointed to the TV. When the commercials came on the she finally responded.

"Hey Baby, where is Mercedes?" She asked.

"Last time I spoke to her she was out and about with Kenya. She should be over here soon." I said.

"What brings you to see me? You only come around when Mercedes tell you I'm cooking."

"Ma, you know that is not true. I just left from over here on Saturday." I said.

"Yeah and you took the rest of my red velvet cake and curry chicken too." She said. "I hope you brought my dishes back."

"Yes Ma'am. They're in the car." I replied. Before she could respond again, I brought the conversation to where I needed it to be. "Well, I came to talk to you about daddy", I said.

She looked at me alert but confused. "What about him?" she asked.

My mom and dad had been together since middle school and they married as soon as they both turned 18 years old. The next year, I was born, that was 26 years ago. On the outside looking in, you would think that they enjoyed the perfect relationship. But that wasn't entirely true. They both had been caught committing adultery. They had their everyday differences and disagreements. They also had major trust issues. But all in all, they never got divorced. They had been living in separate homes since 2005 and throughout these 10 years, dad always provided for her even after he was dead and gone. Mom, is naturally stubborn and she refused to allow him to bribe her with his gifts. She made it her obsession to remain independent.

"Ma, first let me say this. You are fully aware that daddy took me and Mercedes with him around some people, places and things that you did not approve of. So with that being said, we know how he was living. Please don't hold nothing back", she just sat there quiet so I continued, "even if you think it's goin' to hurt, I'mma big girl. Always was. That's what you and daddy taught me" I said.

"What do you want to know Alexus?" She asked.

"I don't know why I feel this way, nor do I have a problem with feeling it. The more I think about him the more I want to do it." She looked at me sideways, how a concerned mother would look at her child.

"Do what Alexus?"
"Find out who killed my daddy and show them how much of a bitch payback really is!" I said.

"You talking about actually killin' somebody?" she asked with an expression of disbelief. I didn't answer.

"You ain't nothing but 26 years old. This not no damn game! Your daddy didn't get where he got in one day. It took him years and a lot of near death experiences to build what he had. You don't know a damn thing about these streets", she stressed, damn near in tears. I stood there with the same feeling, the warmth removed from my heart. Then after about sixty seconds I finally spoke.

"You're right ma. I don't know about these streets but I know a lot about me! The streets is calling me. My daddy took everything serious, always was about his issue and never let nothin' slide, even with his own kids." I said.

She looked at me, something in her expression had changed. "You're serious aren't you?"

"We ain't never been more serious about anything in our lives". Me and mom both looked back to see Mercedes standing just inside the front door. We were so wrapped up in our conversation that we didn't even hear her open the door. I wasn't' even sure how long she was standing there.

"Alexus, you been telling my baby about this finding your daddy's killer bullshit?" mom asked.

"Yeah, we talked about it, but she didn't make no decision for me." Mercedes said, joining us on the couch.

"Oh my God! I'm losing my babies."

"Ma calm down." Mercedes said, "We're waist deep in the street life and if you paid a little more attention than you would have been known that. We got drugs and money. Me and Alexus can damn near shoot the wing off a mosquito and we demand our respect."

"Yeah Ma, but that ain't all to survival, we survive by using our heads, staying one step ahead and making moves without moving." I said.

"So right now, we're just doing our homework." Mercedes told her "and it would be nice if we had your help. We know that daddy kept a lot of things away from you just like he did us but we also know that you know things, things that probably could help us."

"What is all this going to prove?" She finally asked.

"We ain't trying to prove nothin'!" I said. "We just want closure."

"Look, I know a few people, places and things that will point us in the right direction", mom said.

"Us? What do you mean us?" I asked.

She smiled a weak smile and said, "You heard what I said. We all we got. It's us against the world", she paused for a minute to soak in our reaction when we didn't say anything she kept on speaking. "Your daddy dealt with a lot of people from gangstas to police, judges, lawyers and anybody else he could pay to make things go his way. He was the definition of a boss."

We all stayed glued to our conversation for a couple more hours and mom heated up some leftovers that she had from the previous night. We ate and made plans to do our separate research and put the pieces of the puzzle together. I gotta admit, I was shocked but it felt good to have moms playing her part in helping to find out who had killed my dad.

9

Kenya

I've been boomin in Perrine for about 4 months now, whoever Mercedes been getting this work from, got and keep some grade "A-plus" cocaine. I been seeing over 30 racks a month faithfully. Me and Neno been taking turns running the spot but he don't be bringing the numbers that I bring in. A couple of people came here to buy that loud though and I had to check him on that shit before Alexus and Mercedes got wind of it. I respect it though because my cousin is a real go-getter. But I don't run this show, I'm just playing my part.

Damn near my whole family been in the streets at one time or another getting money.

Especially the family that brought me in the game. They tried to put me on plenty of times but I always told them to teach me the game so I could put myself on. They gave me minor errands, took me on some episodes, taught me how to cook, cut and sell crack. Gave me a few custos. It wasn't until a couple of months later that I fell in love with the power of a pistol.

One night me and Neno was out late trying to make a couple more sales and this gray Crown Vic kept coming through the block. We thought it was 'trol but it wasn't, it was some jackboys. I ain't have shit but like four hundred dollars and a couple more pieces. I don't know what Neno had.

Two niggas jumped out in all black and Neno had already peeped it, by the time I looked to my left where he was standing. He was already gone. I was too late and they started shooting in the direction that Neno took off in. I stood there in complete shock until I heard the sound of the tires spinning out.

They didn't even bother me but that was too close of a call for me. I couldn't shake the feeling of being exposed and I had to do something about it. I talked to my uncle Rick about what happened the very next day and he not only got in Neno chest about leaving me but also he gave me a 38 special. At that time I probably couldn't shoot a school bus from five feet away but I kept it with me at all times.

Uncle Rick was cool as fuck. God bless the dead. He was an Americanized Christian converted Muslim and though he was well respected and connected in the street, five times a day he stopped what he was doing and made time for Allah. I remember exactly what he told me when he gave me the gun: "You asked for protection, well I can't sit around and babysit you so I'mma give you this first." He said, pulling out a Quran. "Then I'mma give you this" he said pulling out the 38 special. "Now with this..." referring to the gun, ..."it's rules and rule number one is don't pull it out if you ain't prepared to use it and rule number two is don't let the power of this gun change you. It's for protection not aggression. Allah loves not the aggressor. Its three types of people that tote guns. One who gon' shoot, one who ain't and the one who took too long to shoot."

My phone rang bringing me back from memory lane. "Hello?" I answered without even lookin at the caller ID.

"Bitch where you at?" It was J-Dubb.

"In Perrine waitin on Neno to pull up so I can go." I said.

"Hoe Neno in jail he got caught with two ounces ridin down US1 in Cutter Ridge." He told me.

"Where the fuck he get two ounces from and why he ain't called me?" I asked Jordan.

"I don't know but when Alexus and Mercedes find out they gone wanna know about the two ounces." He said.

"You talked to Alexus and Mercedes yet?" I asked.

"Nah, not since earlier."

"Where you at?" I asked.

"On south Beach, headin to the Fountain Bleu Hotel with my nigga" Jordan said. "I'mma hit you up in the AM when I drop him off."

"Alright, I'm fenna try to find out what's goin" on with Neno, see if he got a bond and shit." I told him.

"If you need some money call and let me know." He said.

"I should be good, if he got a bond it shouldn't be that much." I told him

We talked for another minute and hung up. Jordan sounded like he was getting his dick sucked while he was drivin with J-Dubb, hell it ain't no tellin.

I cancelled my plans and busted a couple more plays at the spot in Perrine while trying to look Neno up on the internet. Apparently he hadn't been booked yet because he wasn't coming up in the system. I called a random bail bonds service and had them look him up ten minutes later they called back and said that he wasn't in the system at all.

Maybe I just had to give it some time.

At 11 pm when the spot slowed down, I closed up and slid to Lincoln Field. When I got over there one of my regulars, Kizzy was coming from our spot. She greeted me with a smile;

"Damn Kenya, I'm glad to see you." She said.

"Yeah my bad girl, I would've been here but some unexpected shit came up", I told her. I liked Kizzy because she was just like me, a female trying to get it in this world. Where the dick get they play and pussy gets played. See us females had to go extra hard to show these niggas that pussy could go just as hard if not harder.

"I need 3 zips" she said following me to the apartment.

Once we got inside she handed me 33 hundred. She also asked me about the beef with the Sr8Drop niggas. "I don't mean to be in your business, but I just don't buy work from you Kenya, I fuck wit you." I just kept quiet trying to see where this was headed.

"One of them niggas from Str8Drop, he ain't no peon either, he up under Peanut like his right hand man. Anyway, he said that some hoe called him all kinds of fuck niggas and pulled a gun on him a couple months ago. Down south in Perrine and he described your car so I know he gotta be taking about you." She said.

She definitely had my undivided attention.

"Sit down" I told her. "So the nigga I pulled my hammer out on is the nigga you fuck with?" I asked.

"So it was you?" she said and started laughing. I looked at her with blood in my eyes and she got the picture.

"Kizzy, it's a cut throat game and I'm waist deep in it on every level. I don't do no fakin' and if I gotta bust my own gun you can believe that bullets gone be flyin'. I know that I was gone have to bump heads with buddy again sooner or later but judging by the info you just gave me I might just be able to run down on him. Who is he?" I asked to see just how far she would go.

"His name is Jock, I met him at the King of Diamonds Strip Club a couple weeks ago" she said.

"Kizzy, I don't know how deep you is in this shit but it ain't no game to play. I take everything serious and I'm always ready to kill or be killed. So if you on my side then be on my side 100%! We cool and all but it's a very thin line between love and hate!" I said making sure she understood.

"Look Kenya you ain't gotta threaten me!" She said on the defensive." I'm the one who offered this info." I love a bitch with balls and Kizzy had just earned a couple points in my book.

"Don't feel no type of way Kizzy and I do appreciate you looking out for me but I just gotta be direct and not beat around the bush." I said in a friendlier tone. "You know where he live at?' I asked.

"He got a few spots he lay his head at, he took me to a house in Carol City behind the Miami Dolphins Stadium, a house in lil Haiti and a duplex down south in Richmond Heights." She said.

"Damn, either he dumb or you got him wrapped around yo finger." I told her

"Girl I put this good pussy on that nigga one time and that was all it took" she said bragging

"When will you be able to show me these spots?" I asked her, while still laughing at her good pussy comment.

Her phone started ringing interrupting us for a minute. She spoke for a couple seconds and hung up

"Probably this weekend" She said answering my last question. "Now what's up with the work? I gotta slide I got people on pause."

I went into our stash spot and gave her the three ounces and her 22 hundred back. "This on the house" I told her.

She looked at me like I was crazy and said, "I told you I fucks with you Kenya. I ain't tell you no info so I can start getting no deals or to play up under you. If I come to get something, I'mma pay for it. Like you said, it's hard on us hoes and it ain't too many real thorough ones left but it's all the way real with me.' She just earned another point.

My phone rang, it must be Neno who I had almost forgot about. I wrapped everything up with Kizzy, let her out the front door and answered the phone, "Hello…"

10

Diamond

Tonight I was chillin' with Gucci from Club Free Money. Lately my time has been split up between this nigga Gucci and Peanut. Juggling' these two niggas was a full time job that Zetta understood because with her it was always business before pleasure.

It's truly amazing how women can penetrate the Teflon layer of these so called gangstas. The power of pussy is kryptonite to these niggas.

Whenever I went out with Gucci I was sure to have a rental car with him because he had me convinced that he was a ghetto king or some shit. We've been "goin' out" for about seven weeks now and for the first month his bodyguard nephews happened to always be in the shadows. I was always on point even though I pretended not to be.

We met at Sunset Mall and enjoyed a nice casual dinner at Buffalo Wild Wings. Afterwards, I followed him back to his house. Gucci had a nice ass crib, ducked off in the suburban Kendall Lakes area. Not far from the Town and Country mall. It was an extravagantly constructed 5 bed 3 bath European styled, two story town house with a two car garage. It was equipped with an indoor/outdoor bar, a gorgeous 90 foot marble tiled pool and a mini movie theater on the first floor and a state of the art recording studio on the second. His crib was decorated with stainless steel appliances and cherry wood furniture that graciously complimented each other. Walking through the front door you could smell the leather of the all-white love seat and sectional that demanded the attention of the formal living room. I had to give credit where it was due, he had a MTV crib.

A week ago was the first time that he had invited me to his crib. I was surprised because I had expected him to propose to me before he showed me where he layed his head. I was convinced that pussy really did have power in it, but with this type of nigga holding out had way more power than benefits.

I knew he kept the cash at this hide away too because I witnessed him count 30 thousand the first time he brought me over. I guess he thought that by showing me his riches, I would be eager to get naked and show him mine. Gucci was very smart and calculated. I knew that by the sterling silver chess board that sat on the dining room table. I worked overtime to stay one move ahead of him.

When I made it home that same night, I told Zetta where this spot was and for the last couple of days, we've been making plans to cash in this lottery ticket.

While Gucci was in the shower, I snuck out the room and unlocked the front door. Zetta had text me and told me to keep him occupied for the next 20 minutes. Ten minutes later he emerged from a foggy but pleasant smelling bathroom, dressed in boxer briefs and a tank top.

Gucci had a nice, muscular, swimmer's body you had to admire; especially without clothes. His boxer briefs left very little room for speculations and I can tell without a doubt that he was very well endowed. He had a six pack that looked like it was sculpted with a million dollar chisel and hammer. "You good sexy?" he asked, unknowingly breaking me out of my pornographic day dream.

Then without waiting on my response, he walked into the closet that contained a secret wall safe.

"Yeah, I'm fine" I said while grabbing my purse and walking into the bathroom to do my own freshening up. Once inside the safety of the bathroom, I texted Zetta to see her location. She was around the corner. I told her to count up to 100 and then come in. After the message was sent I turned the shower on and counted to thirty myself. Then I took my brand-new XD 40 out of my bag and took it off safety, making sure there was already a bullet in the head. While the shower was still running, I walked out of the bathroom gun aimed at the bed where Gucci was sitting with his back turned to me.

"You forgot something?" he asked turning around to see the barrel of my XD 40 aimed at his head, " what the fuck you got goin on?" he asked in a shocked tone.

"Put yo' hands on yo' head and move nice and slow to the floor and lay on your stomach." I said with a no nonsense attitude.

"Girl you betta put that gun up or..."

"Or what nigga?" Zetta asked, steppin into the room wither own identical XD 40 aimed at Gucci. Reality set in as he is face turned to a reflection of a defeat.

"Do what the fuck she told you," Zetta warned through clenched teeth, slappin' him across the head for a push start she then grabbed a pillowcase off the bed as Gucci layed face down on the Persian rug. She threw the pillow case to me. "Clean the safe", she said.

"Y'all don't know who y'all fuckin' wit" he said in a clam but edgy voice "y'all can just walk out of my house and we can pretend this never happened."

"No Mr. Gucci" it really looks like you didn't know who you was fucking with!" I heard Zetta say as I made my way to the safe that to my surprise was already wide ass opened. Without even doing a detailed inventory I raked the contents of the safe into the pillow case. He had money, guns, jewelry, and autographed sport cards in the safe by the time I got done it was spotless.

When I came out the closet Zetta placed two pillows over Gucci's head and nodded for me to send him to his maker. I knew this day was coming and I can't lie, I wasn't really ready but I had to do it. I stood over him, aimed and squeezed the trigger three times. He was dead as soon as the first bullet hit him. I immediately felt my stomach turning.

"Let's go" Zetta yelled grabbing the 40 from my shakin hand. We went through our routine exit clean up and was out the door within 60 seconds.

On our way back home Peanut called saying he wanted to spend time with me tonight but I fed him the "I'm sick" line and promised to call him if I felt any better.

I was an emotional wreck by the time we made it back to the house but somehow I managed to help Zetta count out the 72 thousand dollars in cash. Separate all the jewelry and wipe down all the guns.

We didn't know what to do with the autographed cards so we just put them up in the closet until figured it out.

I took a much needed shower. Standing under 98 degrees of forceful water pressure I decided to take Peanut up on his offer. Maybe I could kill two birds in one night

"Baby" I yelled, while drying off but she didn't answer so I lotion myself up good, and sprayed on my sexual desire perfume. Grabbed my Gucci sheath skirt, halter top with matching Gucci pumps and looking in the fully body mirror; I was dressed to impress.

Tonight I'm cruising in the Lexus LF-NX that I had leased under a fake name. Zetta had used her connects to get me tags and insurance under the alias also so when I was with Peanut, I was Mrs. Kayla Brown. I even added a wedding ring to my outfit for good effects.

When I walked out into the living room Zetta was sitting on the couch in a tank top and some blue and red Ralph Lauren Polo boxers. She had the radio on low, a joint in her mouth and a handful of money that these was counting. She looked up and saw me, I just knew I had messed up her count. She looked me over and sincerely complimented my beauty.

"Damn you fine, turn around and let me see that ass." She said. I spun slowly until my ass was inches away from her face. She gently slapped it and I playfully made it jiggle. "Where you headed at?" she asked.

"Peanut" I said, bending down kissing her on the lips.

"Damn you smell even better than you look" she said. I blushed at the compliment. Then she continued, in her more business like attitude: "You should be wrappin' Peanut up by now".

"He's a lot smarter than I thought he was but just chill. I got him." I told her.

She smiled, "Do you bae, but do it like me. Now go get him", she said slapping me on the ass again. I hopped in the Lexus and headed off to meet Peanut. The sun was about six hours into a deep sleep and about another six hours from waking up. It was a nice night and the slight breeze was a pleasant touch to my skin.

I spoke with Peanut and we both agreed to meet up on South Beach at the Convention Center. Any other day the Convention Center would be packed with tourist, eager to hear the performances of live bands that had traveled from all over the states, but on a Saturday at 12am the Convention Center parking lot was well lit but deserted.

When I finally made it to the Convention Center I saw Peanut sitting on the hood of a burgundy Jaguar C-X17, the car was sitting pretty high on what looked like some 24 inch Ashanti rims trimmed in the same burgundy of the cars exterior.

I parked right next to him and turned my radio down.

"Nice ride" he said apparently shocked that I had pulled up in a 2015 Lexus LF-NX painted a deep bluish lilac color called periwinkle. It had chrome 23 inch Sprewell's spinning counter clockwise. The interior was custom designed Blue's Clues and I only pulled this car out for special occasions. Not many people got a chance to see this car and after today it was going on Craigslist to the highest bidder. I had to make an impression on this nigga and let him know that money wasn't an object I couldn't obtain. It was pure reverse psychology.

"You ridin' pretty handsome ya-self" I said, sincerely impressed. Peanut was casually dressed in a Nautica button up, some crisp Levi's 501 jeans and some buckwheat Timberland boots. He was modestly decorated with a chain on that said,"St8Drp" in black and white diamonds. The gold of his chain and bracelet made the 16 pack in his mouth stand out in the bright lights of the parking lot and the perfect jet black waves in his hair put the icing on the cake. He looked like a celebrity.

"Step out that car for a second Kayla and let me see your outfit." He said, standing up to open my door. I stepped out like a supermodel bitch and his facial expression was complimentary enough for me. I walked to the front of his car and twirled around slowly and seductively giving him a full view of my immaculate physique. He gently grabbed me and pulled me close to him, "Damn, Kayla I gotta have you on my team." He expressed to me while cupping the small of my back with his hands.

All it took was for me to make eye contact with him to know that I had him caught up in my web of lies, lust, hope and eternal damnation. But I still had to keep my game face on. "Peanut," I said, still confined in his embrace. "You know that I'm still legally married", I lied. "And I don't know if I and my husband is gon' to get back together…"

He cut me off. "So where are we headed with this then?" he asked.

"I thought we were getting to know each other. I know that its way more to you than what I've found out so far and its chapters of me that you haven't even began to read yet." I said in my sincerest voice. I almost believed the bullshit I was selling myself.

He started to reply but his phone rang, cutting his words short. He spoke to whoever it was and gave them our exact location. I tensed up slightly because I hated not being in control of the situation and I didn't know who was on the way to meet us. He spoke for a couple more seconds and then hung up. "I feel everything you saying Kayla and I really admire your loyalty and commitment to your husband. I'm not tryin' to rush or force no decision on you. I just want you to know that I'm really feeling you. I admit, at first I thought you were just another one-two step but here it is a month and a half later and I still haven't even gotten a kiss from you".

Just then a champagne gold Cadillac STS pulled into the parking lot and parked right next to Peanut's Jag. The passenger door opened revealing an equally attractive dude, except for his height. He was about 5 foot 8 and dark skinned, which made the 20 pack of golds in his mouth glow like sapphire stones. 'What's up?" he asked as he approached us.

"What's good wit you?" Peanut asked while extending his hand and receiving a gangsta embrace in return. Peanut paused for a second and looked at me. "Kayla this is my main man Jock, and Jock this is my new friend Kayla."

I politely extended my hand to shake Jock's and he gently grabbed and kissed it. "Nice to meet you Kayla" he said. No reply was warranted on my behalf so I just smiled. Peanut and Jock exchanged words for a couple of minutes while I just fell back in the shadows and observed their body language since

I couldn't for the life of me understand the codes that they were speaking in. Jock moved with an authoritive swagger, but I could tell that he looked to Peanut for the real boss decisions.

Through the window of the Cadillac STS I could make out the silhouette of a female in the driver's seat. It looked like she had microbe twist or braids in her hair.

"What y'all getting into tonight?" asked Jock.

"We was just coolin' it, choppin' it up. Why? Who that you got wit you?" Peanut asked.

"Oh that's Kizzy. Y'all wanna slide to Wet Willies wit us and have some drinks?"

Peanut looked to me for an answer. "Shit I could use a drink after a long day at work." I said, more truthfully than they could have imagined. The image of committing my first murder and the thought of Gucci still drowning in his own blood replayed in my mind.

"Where you work at?" Jock asked.

"Oh, I'm a flight attendant slash bar tender." I lied.

"They must pay good!" He said checking out my ride.

I just laughed it off. "I do alright." We all got back in our cars and took the short drive to Wet Willies, a couple blocks down Ocean Ave.

About an hour into our "get together" I knew I had found an alliance in Kizzy. She had a real polished street swag for a female. Her phone must've rang like 8 times and she told the callers that she was either busy or out of the area. She sounded just like Zetta, so I knew her occupation. My female intuition told me that she wasn't really feeling Jock or Peanut although she played her role well. Neither of them noticed but I could tell that Ms. Kizzy had an ulterior motive and well hidden agenda.

We all talked, laughed and ordered drink after drink. Me and Kizzy mainly played over ours and watched them niggas get drunk. At about 4 am we all said our goodbyes and went our separate ways. Before leaving, me and Kizzy made sure to exchange phone numbers.

11

Jordan

Moaning

"Shut Up!"

More uncontrollable moaning

"Take this dick!"

Moaning softens

"Yeah that's right, take this dick! What's my name?!"

"Jordan!" Fantasy managed to say while desperately gasping for air.

"Yeah that's right nigga! Say I got the best dick in the world!"

"You got the best dick in the world Jordan!" Fantasy screamed.

I blessed him with a thirty second break as I turned him on his stomach and spread his legs apart. Then made sure that the neighbors knew my name. I punished him from the back while his dick violently hit between the hotel's mattress and his nicely maintained stomach.

For Fantasy to be a feminine nigga that most would disrespectfully label a "faggot" he had a nicely cut 9 inch dick. He was blessed with the body of an Olympic runner and his nice round firm ass was more delicate than a female's. He maintained his squat work out if nothing else and it showed as we switched positions and he rode my dick.

I am an "oral dominate top" which means that I give and receive oral sex with no boundaries but I would never get fucked or even slightly penetrated. Fantasy on the other hand is what is known as a "submissive bottom" and he'd go about any distance to please the sexual and non-sexual desires of his man.

After about 15 minutes of constant griding, Fantasy turned around and rode me backwards, with his ass towards my face and his hands stretched towards my feet. As I stared up at our reflection in the ceiling mirror, Fantasy did a backwards split and proceeded to slam his ass against my dick.

When I got ready to bust my nut he stopped and started to suck my dick while waiting on this massive volcano to erupt on the surface of his tongue and drip down his chin. When it happened, semen was all over his face and the rest he caught and swallowed. I wasn't done though.

I had popped an ecstasy pill at about 2 am and I was prepared to go until check out time which wasn't until 11 am. I had 6 hours to kill and two more pills to eat. I was beyond motivated because I knew that Fantasy would catch whatever I threw at him. As I got ready to apply more lubricant to

Fantasy's ass my cellphone started to ring. It was Kenya.

"Bitch, do you know what time it is? I answered.

She sounded tired and frustrated, "Jordan I'm sorry fa calling you at this time of morning but you told me to call you if I needed to and I'm calling because I been looking for Neno all over the Miami-Dade County jails website and I can't find no information about him. Then I even called the jail and they said that he was never booked at all."

"I don't know what's up", I told her honestly, "but a friend of mine called me right before I called you earlier and told me that he had saw Neno get handcuffed and placed in the back of an unmarked police car. He even described the Dodge Charger that we bought for Neno and read me the license plate number. I mean, my people ain't got no reason to lie."

"I don't know what's goin' on but I gotta find out before Alexus and Mercedes do or this my ass and more than likely Neno's life." She said.

"Well don't jump to no conclusions, just wait a lil while and see if he pop up in the data base. Shit, shut down both spots for the day if you need to. Call me back if it's an emergency but right now you fuckin' up my vibe," I told her.

"You is so nasty Jordan bye!"

"I love you too Kenya" but before I finished my sentence the line was dead. I took Fantasy up through there a couple more times. We kept on going and going like the energizer bunny and right when the sun started to appear my phone rang again.

"What the fuck?!" I screamed to myself because I was so close to bustin' my nut. But I couldn't let my phone go unanswered. This time it was a number I didn't recognize. "Hello?!" I answered, aggravated but also curious as to who in the fuck was callin me at 7 o'clock in the morning.

"Jordan, I need you to take me to get the car" Neno said.

My mind started to work in over drive because if I was good at anything it was poker. I had to play this hand right because I had some unanswered questions that I needed immediate answers to. And why he chose to call me and not call Kenya first? I chose to play the dumb role on this hand and get his story.

"Hold on Neno" I said as I pressed the record feature on my phone that allowed me to record our conversation. It only took a second and I was hoping that he hadn't grown suspicious.

"What's up?" I asked. "Where you at and where the car at?"

"I'm at the spot in Perrine. I was supposed to take over the spot at 10 o'clock last night but on my way over I got pulled over by the police."

"Yeah?" I asked, giving him a boost to keep going.

"Yeah", he said, "they tore the car up lookin' for drugs and guns but I was ridin' clean because I already knew that they was ridin' hot." He paused for a second and then continued. "I didn't have no license so they ended up writin' me a ticket and towing the car."

"Well at least you ain't go to jail." I said hoping for a reaction but he just stayed quiet. "Where Kenya?" I asked.

"She was supposed to go to the other spot in Lincoln Field when I came to relieve her but I never made it until just now and she ain't here or she ain't answerin' the phone" he said.

I knew that Kenya may have stayed up waiting on word from Neno until her body shut down from lack of sleep and she needed a nice long rest so I agreed to pick Neno up at about 9 am.

"Aight" he said. "I'mma be ready."

"One more thing Neno."

"What's up J-Dubb?" he asked curiously.

"Who phone you callin' me from?"

He paused for a minute and said, "Oh, my phone dead so I called you from my friend phone who dropped me off to the spot."

In my mind I knew that "dropped" meant that his "friend" had completed his or her good deed and they were no longer around but I kept my curiosity to myself and said, "Oh, alright. I'll be there at 9." Then hung up.

I cut my fantasy short with Ms. Fantasy because for one, my dick was no longer hard. Two, my sense for business had overpowered my lust for pleasure. There were too many question marks in the air on Neno and if he wasn't Kenya's cousin then he would've been JFK (dead).

Fantasy worked at a health clinic and was due at work by 12pm. I offered to take him home but he called and was given permission to show up for work at 8:30am. We both hit the shower where I ended up bustin' me a nut for the road. We got dressed and ordered room service. Twenty minutes later we were in my Nissan Maxima in route to the Community Health Institution (CHI).

We made it there with about 10 minutes to spare, we made plans to hook up when my unpredictable schedule was freed up. We exchanged a simple kiss on the lips; he got out and walked into the building. After all the screamin', scratchin' and pullin we had been doing I was surprised that he could walk at all.

As I waited for him to disappear through the sliding glass doors, I recognized a familiar face coming out. It was Mrs. Yolanda, Alexus and Mercedes mom. Mrs. Yolanda looked tough as sandpaper but was as loving as a widowed mother could be. If I'm correct she should be about 44 years old but didn't look a day over 35. From my encounters with her I concluded that she had a no nonsense attitude and she gave me the impression that she was an independent business woman.

I chose not to invade her space this early in the morning and I just observed at a distance. She walked like a woman on a mission while her Louis Vuitton purse slung loosely on her shoulder. She walked to her Hyundai Genesis and placed her purse in the trunk. She got in the driver's seat and after ten seconds she slowly exited the parking lot. I pulled out behind her and when we both made it to the stop sign, something possessed me to take a picture of her license plate. Mrs. Yolanda made a right heading north and I made a left heading south to go see what was up with Neno.

At 8:45 am I was sitting in the drive way of the duplex in Perrine. I waited to see the reaction that Neno would display. The spot was equipped with video cameras that covered every inch of the property and monitors were placed in every room of the duplex. Including the kitchen and bathroom.

The way I see it is if Neno didn't have nothing to hide he would just come out of the house, get in the car and be on our way to the impound lot. On the other hand, if he waited for me to get out and go in the house then it would be a sign that he was using his final second to go over his story again and keep his composure.

I took the time to get my compacted 38 special from under the seat and conceal it in my waistband. After 5 minutes I got out of the car and unlocked the door with the key that we all had. I was invited by the smell of bacon with a light hint of burned plastic. Neno was in the kitchen putting grits, eggs and bacon in a bowl and he had a joint hanging from his lips.

"You want some?" he said, while quickly putting the joint in the ashtray.

"Nah, I already ate, but hurry up because I got some shit to do."

"Oh I didn't even see you out there" and then he looked at his watch "you 10 minutes early and I ain't expect you to be on time."

I looked over at the 15 inch monitor that showed my car in the driveway. How the fuck he didn't know I was in the driveway for a whole 5 minutes? But I didn't say shit. It didn't escape my attention that Neno had some form of cocaine inside his joint neither. I knew what cocaine smelled like when mixed with marijuana and set on fire, burned plastic. As far as I was concerned Neno was water under the bridge and Kenya was going to have to tend to her responsibility real quick.

I took Neno to get the car from the impound lot and along the way he tried to feed me the same bullshit story. I played along with him while debating whether to kill him now or kill him later. He was playing with my intelligence and I wasn't up for the fuckery. I decided to give him time, not because I gave a fuck about sending him to hell but I gave a fuck about Kenya. I was a King amongst Queens and I made a vow to be loyal to them since day one.

12

Alexus

I slid the 2015 smoke gray Chrysler 300 straight from the rental car company through a couple hoods, just checking out the scene for business expansions. My first tour was through the very dangerous but profitable Over Town. I spotted some ideal apartments on 18th street and N.W 2nd Court. Then through the 40's, I eventually ended up sliding through Wynwood, Allapattah, Lil Haiti, Edison Projects, Victory Homes Projects, the Pork-n-Bean projects, Brown Subs, as far as even Lil Havana.

I decided on the potential business establishments. The apartments in Over Town, a building directly across the street from the Brownsville Metro Rail Station and a duplex on the back side of the Pork-N-Beans.

I attempted to make a few calls to draft a few more soldiers. I called Kenya first and didn't get an answer which was kind of strange and unexpected. Then Jordan who answered but sounded like he hadn't any sleep and was still preoccupied at the moment. I called Neno, who I don't regularly call and his phone went straight to the voice mail. I hung and tried again, same thing. I knew that I could always depend on Kenya and J-Dubb so I didn't sweat it too much but Neno knew to have his work phone on at all times and I was going to have to check him on that later.

I was looking to expand our operation because Mercedes had landed us a plug that had more than enough supply for our demand. Hell, the plug was demanding that we buy more supply and in return the numbers would come down a whole 15 percent. Kenya had the spots in Perrine and Lincoln Field boomin' and she seemed to be doing a good job of managing both of them. Meanwhile while me and Mercedes did the more executive task of establishing potential plugs and wholesale buyers. Jordan was playing his role well, making moves on the phone and he was there to apply pressure when it was needed. Neno was Kenya's fill-in man under close supervision and personal authority.

Kenya and I had briefly discussed putting Kizzy on our team. I knew of Kizzy, we crossed each other's paths in passing a few times. I had been hearing her name more and more, but never on no flaw shit. If Kenya was willing to vouch for her then I had no doubt in my mind but that was a decision for a later date.

I really had no room to complain because other than our beef with them Str8Drop niggas everything has been more than good. My personal phone rang interrupting my thoughts. It had to be somebody that was either family or a close friend because only a selected few had my personal number. I answered without looking because I was afraid that I would either miss the call or crash trying to check the caller ID. "Hello?" I answered.

"Come to the castle, its important" I heard mom's voice say, then the call was disconnected.

"Hello?" I said, obviously to myself. It had to be important because if not she would have let me know what was up right then and there. Ever since me, her and Mercedes had that discussion at her house a couple weeks ago, one of us was always at the castle doing our own private investigation.

I cancelled my plans and instead of heading south to Perrine I headed north on I-95 to Aventura. The Aventura Police are known for harassing young people in expensive looking luxury vehicles so I cautiously and carefully maneuvered through the streets. I reached my destination about 35 minutes later pulling up to the elegant white bar gates that protected the castle.

The "Castle" is an 8 bedroom, 4bath 3 story house built and specifically customized for Aretha Franklin herself in the late 1970's. It was equipped with a 4 car garage, tennis court, a 12 seat movie theater and a newly renovated Olympic style swimming pool. Spaciously built on 4 acres of land and last I checked favored in the community; worth $3.75 Million dollars.

My dad had always been strict on security. The castle had a total of 28 high definition, motion censored surveillance cameras. They covered damn near every inch of the property leaving very little room for blind spots; complete with state of the art technology security features. The property was accessible by fingerprint and voice analysis. In order for an intruder to gain access he or she not only had to choose the right finger and cut it off but also steal your voice box as well, which was virtually physically and impossible. I placed my index finger on the finger print reader and spoke into the voice analyzer, the gate slowly and smoothly slid open.

As I eased around the maroon tiled circular driveway, I parked behind my mom's 2015 Hyundai Genesis. She had recently purchased the limited edition car at an auction and had it painted a sea foam green. I stepped out of my car greeted by the sun with a sticky and humid heat. I rushed to the cherry wood double doors and wiped the droplets of sweat that threatened to mess up my makeup. I allowed my fingerprint to be scanned once more while speaking my name into the V.A. system again listening as the motor hummed and the doors slowly opened.

I walked into the magnificently decorated formal living room. The room was bathed in a peach pastel that blended extremely well with the tropical accessories adorned throughout the space. The fresh floral arrangements perfumed the air. On the far wall was a floor to ceiling mirror that covering the entire length of it giving you the false perception that the room was twice as big as it was. Mom's purse was sitting on the couch.

"I'm in the security office" Mom's voice blared over the intercom, causing me to flinch slightly. Taking the escalator up to the second floor I followed the hall to the end where the security office sat. Before my dad died this place was lively and vibrant with people. On occasions he would have his business partners, associates, and employees over for casual dinners. Celebrating their underworld business achievements. He had an entire staff for the castle; which included a housekeeper, mechanic, chef, and landscaping maintenance crews. Since his death though, only the housekeeper remained at the castle basically maintaining everything herself.

As I approached the door of the security office the motion sensor signaled the door to open and it did, slowly. My mom didn't even bother turning around and I could tell that she was in the process of deep contemplation. I eased behind her and watched her watch my dad go to a part of the castle that we didn't even know existed. "Where is that? And why is this my first time seeing it?" I asked her.

"The answer to your first question is I have no idea and I have never seen it either." Mom answered "but it looks like a hidden basement, I been watching this all day and that's the reason I called you. I need you to help me find it. "

"Ma, it shouldn't be too hard, all we have to do is track that camera and follow dad," I told her. "Call my phone and lead me to where dad went."

Mom led me to the den where dad spent a lot of time reading and relaxing. He had personalized the room to his liking, his own little man cave. The perimeter of the den was lined with shelves filled with books. There were two tables in the den, one used to eat on and the other held chess board with an unfinished game. I noticed the dust on the table which gave me the conclusion that it hadn't been touched since dad died. I grew curious because from my knowledge the den was off limits to everybody. I made a mental note to see what I could do to have the board and pieces finger printed and then I moved on. I listened as mom called out the directions over the phone. They led me over to the bookshelf on the far wall. Dust covered the shelf like a fine cotton blanket.

"Stop right there" she said through the phone. "Now on the second to last shelf count the fifth book from left to right."

"Okay ma, it's the 48 laws of Power book that dad always kept in his car."

"No, not that one I'm sorry it's the 6th book" she said.

"The Mysteries of Mankind" I said as I read the cover and removed the book from the shelf. I noticed a knob on the wall where the book had been. I turned the knob and automatically heard a click come from the opposite wall. I put the phone down, curiously and cautiously walked towards the wall which had mechanically transformed itself into a four inch thick stainless steel door. The door didn't have a handle or knob which left me clueless as how to open it, but not for long. I got within two feet of the door, I heard the soft hum of an electric motor and an eye analyzer slowly came out. The digital words on the screen said, "Place eyes here."

Against my better judgement, I followed the direction and placed my eyes directly on the eye ports. About 5 seconds later a computerized voice said, "Thank you, please step back." I took a couple steps back not knowing what to expect but too curious to let whatever happens next deter my mission. As the door slowly opened there's room with a desk, touchscreen computer and wall panel filled with buttons. I powered on the computer and waited for or to boot up while scanning the buttons on the wall panel. Finding the one that said security office intercom and pressed it.

"Ma, can you hear me?" I asked. A second later she responded.

"Yes, loud and clear but after you went into that door I lost all visual of you."

"That's because there are no cameras in here, there's a computer though and it looks like about 3 another rooms beyond this one" I told her.

"Check them out Alexus but please be careful."

"I will, can you call Mercedes and tell her to get here right away?" I asked.

"I already did" she said. "She should be here in about 15 minutes."

As I cautiously moved down the darkened corridor of the basement I notice that everything is tiled in smoke gray marble and the doors were identical to the first stainless steel one. There were three different doors to what I assumed were the separate rooms or storage areas. All three rooms had clipboards hanging on the walls outside the heavy steel doors. Each contained logs with dates and times. The entries were extensive and they were all in my dad's unique handwriting. The last entry was on April 14, 2013, exactly two days before he was killed. That was also exactly 19 months ago.

As I approached the first door the access process began and the eye analyzer appeared. After 5 seconds the room door opened just as the first had followed by the computerized voice saying "Thank you".

The door opened I was immediately greeted with the overwhelming smell of nail polish remover. I covered my nose instinctively and walked in; the room had the same marble tiles as the hall. In the middle of the room sat what looked like a 50 gallon plastic water tank. As I got closer to the only object in the room and looked in, there were ten packages the size of a shoe boxes wrapped in some sort of aluminum wrapper. Without to opening them, I knew what they were. I exited the room and the door automatically closed. Before I could open the other rooms I heard the first hidden door slide open and Mercedes walked in with a confused expression painted on her face.

"What the fuck is all this?" she asked.

"Another one of dad's brilliant plans and well kept secrets", I told her turning my attention to the computer screen.

"What's in these rooms?" she asked.

"Well-being that the security system recognized your eyes, I believe that dad wanted you to see for yourself." I told her. I clicked a few buttons on the computer using my name and birthday as the username and password and to my surprise the home screen popped up with a picture of me and my dad on it. There was one file showing on the computer's desktop titled Alexus. I clicked on the folder icon and a video started playing.

The date of the original recording said, March 18th 2013. A couple weeks before my dad died. As the video started to show activity Mercedes emerge from the hidden room holding one of the ten packages wrapped in aluminum. She started to speak but dad's voice caught her words in her throat turning her attention to the video.

Dad was in the video sitting in his den and facing a camera that he had set up himself. He was dressed finely in a cream colored, double breasted 3-piece Armani tuxedo. The video was cut didn't show his feet but I could imagine he had on his signature 1200 dollar Stacy Adams. The only person I've ever saw wear a suit better than my dad was probably Steve Harvey even still, my dad gave him a fun for his money. After a couple of second we watched my dad pour himself a glass of his favorite wine imported from Luxembourg, France in the late 1960s. He then looked directly at the camera and took a sip; using his handkerchief to wipe his mouth he began to speak.

"Look at you Alexus, my young gorgeous and intelligent princess. I'm not sure how long it took you but I was very sure that you would eventually find this room and access my computer. Now that I'm gone only you and my other wonderful daughter Mercedes have access to this room. If anybody else tries to break into this area it will immediately explode into flames. I always maintained security because I understood that with money comes power and with power came respect, yet the respect tends to bring about fear and envy. I achieved my success only after out smarting my adversaries and conquering death 3 times". He paused and took a sip from his glass.

"My intentions are not to brag but to inform you that I am a calculated man if nothing else. I know that you and your sister stole a key of cocaine from me in 2011. I've always known." He paused and I and Mercedes glanced at each other, he continued. "Even before you took it, I knew that you both would most likely follow in my footsteps of success. I know that over the last couple of years, I've allowed business to consume my time and for that I sincerely apologize. I also want you to know that the separation of me and your mother had nothing to do with you two at all. I've ignored and wronged her several times and at the end she just couldn't forgive me. I pray that one day she will. Since the day you took it upon yourselves to deprive me of 36 ounces of cocaine, I hired a private team of bodyguards to protect you and I have known about most of your business transactions. I must say that I am impressed. I have left you and Mercedes a gift in room 1. Also room 2 is an identical to the first but the only object in it is a notebook filled with information. I'm sure that you'll use the connects well and honor your Father. Listen Alexus", he said while sitting up and getting closer to the camera,

"...nothing in life is free and some things can even cost you your life. You must build your dreams or someone will hire you to build theirs". He then relaxed a bit and continued speaking.

"In the third room is your protection. You must protect yourself at all times because no one will value your life like you. I didn't have mind enough to protect myself in many ways and the end results do show. Materialistic things only bring a temporary sense of joy, so don't forget to do things and embrace the people that promise permanent bliss. I've been fighting a losing battle for about 2 decades now and I feel as if my time to depart from this world is gonna be sooner than later. I advise you and Mercedes to continue to build your own empire and not to continue mine. I also advise you to not become so rich so that all you have is money. I love you both dearly and I am confident that you will grow the level of success that I have never achieved". He put the index finger of his right hand up and closed his eyes, "Ashadu In-la Ilaha Il-allah. Ashadu anna Muhammadar Rasulullah". Then using the remote control to stop the recording the screen went black.

We filled my mom in on a few things but left out the info that she didn't need to know. She was complaining of not feeling well and after a while longer she left, headed for her own house. Me and Mercedes again returned to the private basement and checked the other two rooms.

In room two there was a small antique desk placed in the middle of the floor. On top of it lay a composition book with names, numbers and addresses. Dad's business partners and associates information. The list included everyone from law enforcement to government officials and anybody else needed in order to build and maintain an illegal empire. I kept seeing the name Devin, I noticed that dad put a lot of effort in investigating and describing who this Devin dude was. In the descriptions, dad used words like determined, calculated, intelligent, and loyal. I made a mental note to double back and find out more about Devin and then me and Mercedes moved to room three.

In room three there was enough guns to go to war with Russia. In fact there were a variety of guns from Russia. A M-16 to a Russian made AK-47. There were 7 hand guns and 6 assault rifles. There was an inventory sheet for the guns and sufficient ammunition for each. Dad had a bullet proof vest, samurai sword, brass knuckles; switch blades and razors all lined up across a well-organized shelf. In the last drawer was a Holy Quran by Yusuf Ali and a King James Version of the Holy Bible. Dad had said that this room was for protection and he meant it to the fullest.

Me and Mercedes stayed to the castle from 3pm to almost midnight. The housekeeper was an older lady by the name of Ms. Gloria and we always called her Glo for short. She lived in the pool house and had access to only public rooms of the house. She made us her special homemade spaghetti and garlic bread so we shared a nice dinner with her. We both made plans to discuss our next move with Kenya and Jordan. We locked up the house and each went to our respective homes.

On my ride home this Devin dude kept popping up in my head and I make sure to remind myself to do a full investigation on him after I get the chess board and pieces fingerprinted.

13

Mercedes

I left the castle feeling like Queens Up had just hit the lotto. I was in the mood to celebrate and I headed to my man's house to have an exclusive celebration party, just the two of us.

Me and J.T. been together for 5 years, since I was 19 and he was 26. J.T isn't the cream of the crop but when I met him he treated me like royalty and in return I gave him my loyalty. He is about 6 feet 3 inches tall and weighs close to 275lbs. He played defensive right nose guard for the Florida Gators but injured his knee before he could go pro. Even with his athletic ability he was more fat than muscle but I remained loyal, even though I got opportunities to have a better man.

I took I-95 south and then the I-12 west and got off in Doral, after a 35 minute drive from the castle I was pulling up to J.T's crib. As I pulled up unannounced, I noticed a maroon 2011 Nissan Maxima that I had never seen before and I just knew that we were about to have a problem. I had my own key and I let myself in. As soon as I stepped in, I heard moaning and the distinguished sound of a head board hitting the wall. In the living room I took off all my clothes except my Victoria's Secret lingerie and my Prada pumps. Then I pulled my chrome .380 out of my matching Prada purse.

I quickly checked myself out in the full body mirror and walked down the hall to J.T's room. I eased the door open quietly; they didn't even know I was there. He was laying on his back and she was riding him cow girl style. I took the .380 and tapped loudly on the wall. They both flinched and turned around in a shocked. I was standing there looking like a mix between Buffy the Body and one of Charlie's Angels.

She jumped off of J.T. and out the bed while looking for her clothes in one swift move. Fumbling to put on the ones she found. I cocked back the gun, she froze and looked at me. J.T just layed there because he already knew how stupid I could be.
I aimed the gun at her "what's your name?" I asked with a hostile attitude.

"Jackie" she said in a shaky voice.

"Get on your knees right now!" I said while holding the gun with two hands for a better aim. She started crying but she did just as I commanded. As I walked toward her, her eyes widen clearly terrified and uncertain of my next move. J.T. just layed there waiting on my instructions to him. When I got right in front of Jackie she started to tremble and I put the gun to her head. She was eye level with my waistline and still trembling. I pulled my Victoria Secret panties to the side and exposed my freshly shaved pussy.

"Lick this pussy" I told her while shoving the gun harder into her temple. Her eyes opened wider as she realized what I said.

"Huh?" she managed to mumble.
From the corner of my eye I notice J.T eye's pop out as well.

"You heard me hoe! Since you wanna be a hoe and fuck my man you gone fuck me too! Now eat this pussy!" I said, grabbing her hair with my free hand. I'm not sure if she had ever performed oral sex on a female but she went to work on me. She was penetrating my pussy with her tongue and all. When she was in the groove I pointed my 380 at J.T.

"Get the fuck over here now fuck nigga!" It wasn't a request, it was a command and he understood that. He got out of the bed and walked over to us. While Jackie ate my pussy, I took one leg and placed it on the bed and spread my ass cheeks with the hand that was previously holding Jackie's hair. I didn't have to speak J.T knew what time it was and he got on his knees and ate my ass. He licked up and down slowly as I rocked back and forth between his tongue and Jackie's. Then he licked faster and faster. When he tried to taste my insides, I exploded an orgasm all over Jackie's face. I was just getting started.

    I stopped both of them and pushed J.T on the bed. As he lay on his back, I climbed on top of him and slowly slid down on his 11 inch dick. Then I motioned for Jackie to come behind me. I layed down on J.T's chest and used my free hand to spread my ass. J.T. moved my hand and used his own to spread my ass open. Jackie got on her hands and knees while on the bed and proceeded to eat my ass while I rode my man's dick. After having two orgasms I stopped them and I got out of the bed.

I got dressed without saying a word and hopped in my BMW and pulled off. As I jumped back on the 112east J.T called my phone at least 8 times. I didn't answer because deep down inside I was really hurting. I loved J.T to death and no I wasn't going to leave him, but I couldn't understand why he always cheated on me. Look at me, I'm 5'8 165 pounds thick, hazel brown skinned, shoulder length hair and very independent. What more could he ask for? I proved my faithfulness and loyalty to him over and over again. Before I realized it, I had shed a dozen tears.

It was about 1:30am, I wasn't ready to go home so instead I took the turnpike to Perrine to check on our investment. When I pulled up to the spot Neno was outside talking to some niggas in a turquoise Infiniti Truck. He didn't notice me because he was used to seeing me in my 2015 Chevy Impala. When I got out of the car they both looked in my direction.

"What's goin" on over here Neno?" I asked, not hiding my curiosity. Before I got close enough to see who the niggas were the driver put the truck in gear and pulled off. "Who the fuck was that?" I asked Neno.

"What's up Mercedes? That was one my custos. He straight. He just be paranoid and he didn't know who you was." Neno told me.

Although Neno was calm and collected. What he told me just didn't sit well with me. Clearly ain't nobody pullin' up in a brand new Infinity to rob or kill nobody and I ain't never saw the police hop out of one either. Also it just seemed that Neno seemed was little bit too calm and collected. I damn sure took note that my spider bitch senses kicked in.

"You know we got a meeting in the morning at Denny's on 36th street and Biscayne Blvd?" I asked.

"Yeah Kenya told me."

"Alright, make sure you on time or Alexus is gone trip." I told him. "Is everything good over here?" I asked.

"Yeah, everything good. I still got a couple half ounces left."

"Okay, I was just stopping by cause I was in the area", I lied then continued. "Try to stay in the shadows and don't have nobody hanging out around here. This ain't no chill spot."

"I'll remember that" he said walking back to the duplex

I got back in my car and drove a few blocks to Homestead Avenue. I went to the 24 hour Arab store and got me a cranberry juice. After about five minutes I doubled back to the spot and guess what the fuck I saw? That same fuckin' Infiniti truck!

My first mind was to pull by Tek 9 from under the seat and get some direct understanding but my better judgement kicked in and I knew that patience was really a virtue. In my heart I could feel like something was going on with Neno so I called Kenya.

"What's up?" she answered on the first ring.

"Where you at?" I asked.

"Still at the spot in Lincoln Field."

"Oh, I'm on my way over there." I told her.

"Alright, but be careful cause the police was swarmin' earlier." She warned me.

"Alright" I said before hanging up.

It was a 35 minute drive but because it was almost 3 in the morning I made it there in 20 minutes. When I got there I unlocked the door with my key and walked in knowing Kenya had already saw me pull up from her well hidden video cameras.

"What's up Mercedes?" Kenya greeted.

"Same shit, what's good wit you?" I asked.

"Bitch I done been through it all and it ain't shit that I can't handle" she said and asked, "What brings you to the jungle at 3 in the morning?"

"Neno." I said, without realizing that the words actually left my mouth.

"Neno?" she asked looking real confused. I could tell that she was in the process of putting up some ounces so I gave her a second to finish up and she came and sat next to me on the couch.

"What about Neno?" She asked.

"I don't know but that's what I came to ask you because he is your responsibility first and your cousin second."

"Well, two days ago", she started "Jordan called me and said that Neno had got arrested for havin' two ounces of coke in his car. Jordan got the info from somebody he knew. But when I called the bailsman and looked him up on the internet he never showed up in the system. Then early yesterday morning he showed up to the spot in Perrine and said that he never got arrested. I double checked the inventory and everything was on point so I didn't bother to alert you and Alexus because it seemed to just be a mix up."

"Girl, I trust your judgement but keep your ears open. Don't let the blood cloud your eyes. I done seen blood choke the life out of some people." I told her.

"Yeah you right and I will be on point about that from now on."

"Thank you! You know you like my sister from another mother and I got yo back like yo t-shirt" I said.

"Oh shit, while you here I might was well fill you in." she began. "My home girl Kizzy gave me the word on them Str8Drop niggas. Remember I told you that I pulled my piece out on one of them niggas in Perrine a couple months ago?"

"Yeah I remember that."

"Okay well come to find out that was Peanuts second in command soldier. His name is Jock and my home girl Kizzy been fuckin' wit him for a couple of weeks now."

"And?" I asked hoping she'd get to the point.

"And!" Kizzy is our plug to run down on them niggas" she said. The earlier scene with Neno replayed in my mind, I made a mental note to check further into what he had going on.

"Okay, we'll cross that bridge when we get to it." I told her then changed the subject. I made sure Kenya had enough work to last her until after the meeting and prepared to leave. The clock had struck 4am and I needed to get at least 5 hours of sleep if I was going to be any good at the meeting. We said our goodbyes and I exited the apartment headed for my BMW.

As I descended the stairs my phone started ringing, it was J.T. At first I wasn't going to even answer but I knew that if I didn't he would just keep calling and calling. Distracted by my phone and physically exhausted, I failed to see or sense the nigga who was hiding under the stairs until it was too late.

A figure dressed in all black with a black ski-mask jumped out from the shadows and attempted to grab my arm. Out of pure reflexes I managed to push him off balance and take off running. Without looking back I could hear him groan from the fall and scrambling to get back up. A second or two later I heard gun shots and felt the bullets intruding on the air around me. I hit the ground face first, feeling as though I had been pushed. When I managed to look back the figure was running towards me. Being completely powerless to do anything else. I heard myself saying a prayer. Before he could reach me, I heard a different set of gun shots. The shots were rapid and had to be coming from an automatic assault rifle. The figure who was running towards me wisely aborted his mission and ran for cover behind the row of the cars in the parking lot.

My brain was demanding my hand to reach inside my handbag for my 380 but my arm or hand wasn't receiving the signal. In the next split second I see Kenya running, shooting, ducking, and dodging, looking like Angelina Jolie in that movie Mr. and Mrs. Smith. I lay there on the ground unable to move and listened to their exchange of gunfire. After about 30 seconds the shooting ceased and Kenya ran over to me.

"Are you alright?" She asked, while looking me over. "Damn you got hit." She said. After the shooting ceased people started looking out their windows and a few even came outside. Sirens could be heard in the distance.

"I'm straight help me up." I told her. "Then go and put that gun up."

"Bitch, I'm not leaving you out here." She said, as she helped me up. A task that was easier said than done. She walked me back to the building and I sat on the stairs. I could see blood running down my leg and back arm.

"Alright, I'm good now go and put that gun up and come back." I told her as I pulled out my registered 380 from my hand bag. She didn't respond, she just ran upstairs.

The police and ambulance arrived at the same time and I was rushed to Jackson Memorial Hospital. Although the paramedics whispered among themselves. I could tell they were afraid that I would bleed to death. I drifted into a deep black sea of unconsciousness.

When I woke up a couple hours later I could see the sun shining through the hospital's curtains. Mom, J.T Alexus and Kenya were all present in my room. When they noticed my eyes were open they all gathered around and asked the obvious questions. I was tired and my mouth was dry. I could barely speak so I didn't even try to.

After hearing the relief of my family and friends, I fell asleep. Later when I awoke again it was night and only Alexus there.

"What's up sis?" I managed to get out somehow. Alexus walked over to the side of my hospital bed and rubbed my hand. I could see the genuine worry in her eyes.

"Shit, I'm just glad that you're okay" she began, "whoever that was shootin' at you was aiming at you was aiming to kill and if it wasn't for Kenya I'd be planning yo' funeral right now." I caught a glimpse of the compassionate and protective big sister that I remembered as a kid. A second later I caught the chills when I looked into her eyes. Her eyes were nothing but a window to her cold heart and treacherous soul.

I tried to speak but couldn't due to the emotions swelling up in my throat. I watched as Alexus pulled a photo out of her back pocket.

"One of the neighbors found this picture next to the car that the shooter ran behind." She said while handing it to me. It was a photo of us at our dad's funeral.

"Where did the shooter get this?" I managed to whisper.

"My guess, it could have come from anybody. Dad had close to a thousand people at his funeral. My real concern is the fact that we are both together on this picture, so whoever it was that tried to kill you must be coming after me next." Alexus said.

I could see blood in her eyes. She was physically present in my hospital room but her mind was far from here. Alexus took after our dad and she could play chess with the best of the best. She didn't have to speak for me to know what was on her mind. It wouldn't have made any sense of me to try to calm her emotions at this point. And I wasn't sure

I wanted to because if the shoe was on the other foot I'd feel the same.

"Did you speak to the doctor?" I asked her.

"Yeah, she said the she recommended you stay just for observation purposes because you lost a lot of blood."

"I can't….." I began to say and she cut me off.

"You ain't got no choice. Don't be stupid! I called in a few favors and hired you an around the clock set of bodyguards. I gotta go put my ear in these streets. Somebody gone answer my questions and I ain't gon' sleep until they do." She said as she started gathering her things to leave.

"Be safe Alexus please." I said as a lonely tear escaped my eye.

"Only way I know how to be safe is to erase all threats." She said as she walked out and closed the door.

14

Zetta

Club Exotic is a strip joint in the heart of downtown Miami. For it to be a rather small establishment, Club Exotic was the place to be on a Thursday night. The whole plaza where it was located was packed with some of everybody. Cars were parked all on the sidewalk on both sides of the street. Also, in the plaza was a 24-hour corner convenience/liquor store.

I really don't come to Club Exotic because of that ghetto ass store filled with the neighborhood ghetto bitches but I didn't feel like driving all the way to the beach and Club Rolex was shut down for the night due to somebody shooting. Sitting in my Dodge

Challenger rolling a joint showing off my 23inch deep dish Ashanti rims I just had put on. Done rolling up, I got out with my bottle of Remy and poured myself a cup, sitting the bottle on the hood of the car I posted on the sidewalk with no intention of going inside the club. I never went anywhere that my glock 40 couldn't go.

I just vibed to the music coming from my car and observed my surroundings I saw a couple fine hoes, a couple jazzy bitches, and then the regular old hood tramps. The air was thick with smoke from probably every drug that would catch a flame. It felt like home to me. I heard my name and looked in the direction it came from while on my way to my passenger seat where I had my glock 40, cocked and off safety. I stopped in my tracks when I realized that it was my plug Devin.

He was different tonight, instead of being casually dressed in Polo, Nautica, or Abercrombie and Fitch he was impressively decked out in a blue, black and white Jordan outfit. He was Jordan from head to toe including his socks. He had a platinum Rolex on his left wrist and a wedding ring with a diamond the size of a nickel. He wore a moderate sized chain but kept it concealed inside his shirt.

"What's up fam?" I greeted as he approached me. "This don't look like the type of spot you would hang at" I said speaking my thoughts out loud.

"It ain't gangsta, I'm just passin through." He said.

"You want a drink?" I asked pointing at the Remy.

"Nah, I only drink champagne. That hard liquor ain't good fa you."

"Yeah, I only drink occasionally." I said.

"I just opened my own strip club and I could use a good assistant if you interested. I know more about you than you think I do and I respect the game at all angles."

He caught me off guard. "What you been spyin' on me nigga?" I asked in a playful manner but dead serious.

"You buy work from me and you're sort of like my unofficial business partner, so yes. I must stay informed about anybody that got even the smallest connection to me. I been in the game since I was 13 and I ain't survive these 17 years without studying and doing my homework. I been to jail one time in 17 years and that was all it took. Either play the game right or don't play it at all." He said.

I just listened until he was done because I knew bullshit when I heard it and Devin was far from a bullshitter. I assumed that he knew about all my dealings and being that he was asking me to be his assistant I was convinced that he didn't disapprove.

After a brief pause he continued to speak. "Listen Zetta, if you wonderin' do you have my approval of yo' extracurricular activities then the answer is fuck NO!"

I damn near choked on my Remy. What the fuck is this nigga a spy and a mind reader?

"Not because I give a fuck about them niggas because I don't, you on the other hand have the potential to run circles around most of these niggas in the game at a far less risk because you're female and no one will see you comin'."

"So what club do you own?" I asked with interest.

He smiled and finally said, "Club Free Money."

"I heard a lot about Club Free Money but I haven't been there yet."

"I know but Diamond was there at the grand opening and caught her a pretty big fish." He said. Damn this nigga dangerous. "Anyways I got some moves to make, I just stopped by because my 7th sense told me I would find you here. You got my number so hit me up and we can see about getting you that official promotion."

"Yeah I'mma get at you about that real soon." I said not overlooking the fact that he knew where to find me when I had never planned on being here. We dapped each other up and he walked into the liquor store.

After he went in the store I scanned my surroundings. I saw some niggas checking Devin out like they was up to something so I kept an eye on them while moving closer to my glock 40 and starting my car up. Dust kicked up as the powerful motor came to life. One of the dudes went over to a black Cadillac Escalade and reached under the seat pulling out some sort of hand gun. I inched a little closer to them so if they made a move I wouldn't be far away.

From the other end of the parking lot I heard a commotion but before turning to check it out, I made a visual contact that Devin was still in the store talking to the owner. The guy was an older Arab man, Devin and him looked like old friends reunited.

When I turned toward the commotion it was some hoes going blow for blow probably over some gossip or some baby daddy drama. I didn't let it distract me and I kept my eyes glued to these niggas in the Escalade.

Devin finally came out the store with a bottle of champagne in hand. "Don't forget to holla at me." He said to the older man then walked off.

As I saw the niggas getting out of the Escalade I pick up my glock 40 and screamed out to Devin who turned around startled.

"What's up?" he asked while looking in the direction of where I had my gun pointed. Then he smiled. He said, "I knew you were the real one, but with my guidance and education you could own these streets. Put yo gun away. They with me.... 24 hours 7 days a week. Even when you can't see them sort of like a guardian angel." After Devin exited the parking lot on his royal blue Kawasaki Ninja bike, I got in my car and headed home.

Diamond was already asleep and I undressed and eased in the bed beside her. I wrapped my arms around her midsection and pulled myself to the warmness of her body. She moved a bit, acknowledging that I was home and within minutes I was dreaming of swimming in a pool of money while Devin flipped some burgers on a barbecue grill in never never land.

I got up around 9am the next day because my phone kept ringing, making it impossible for me to sleep. I had Diamond enroll in a college course for Business Administration at Miami Dade Community College. She had left about an hour earlier to make it her first day on time.

I hit the streets running and met up with L.J he had all my money and was in need of some more mango Kush. I already had what he needed and I wondered if Devin was watching me at this very minute and how much did he really know?

Around 12:30, Diamond texted me and asked me to bring her lunch. I stopped at TGI Friday's and picked up her favorite meal. On the way to the college I stopped and purchased a dozen white roses from an independent vendor on the side of the road. I respect all hustles.

When I made it to the college Diamond was there sitting in my Infiniti Truck with another girl. I pulled directly in front of the truck and put my hazard lights on. When I walked to the driver's window she rolled it down and gave me a kiss on the lips then she introduced me to her friend.

"Zetta, this is Kizzy who I was telling you about and Kizzy this is my baby." I politely spoke with Kizzy and apologized for not bringing her a plate too. Then I traded cars with Diamond leaving her my pink and purple 2015 Dodge Challenger and hit up the city again.

That's the life when you out here in the streets. My phone won't stop ringing. I got custos all over

Miami and I'm constantly on the move. With a connect like Devin, ain't no way I could go wrong. He keep some grade "A" strains of Mary Jane.

I had been thinking about the proposition that Devin had threw in my lap last night. I was feeling being his assistant at Club Free Money because it meant I could have a legit income to cover up all this illegitimate money me and Diamond were spending. Even though I already had my answer I planned to wait it out because if I answer too quick I'll look too eager, then again if I took too long I'd look indecisive.

My phone rung, breaking my train of thought. I took my eyes off the road for a second and looked at the caller ID, it was Devin. "Yeah?" I answered trying not to sound too expectant.

I didn't get no response and the phone call was disconnected. A second later he called again.

"What's up Devin?" I answered.

"That's better" he said "What kind of business person answers their phone talking about yeah?" he said, asking a rhetorical question. I didn't answer just listened. "Listen Zetta, in order to become who you wanna be, you gotta start thinking like who you wanna be. But anyways, I didn't call you to lecture you. I called to invite you and your significant other to enjoy a business dinner with me tonight at the Paris Hilton Hotel on South Beach at 6:30pm."

15

Alexus

"Are you sure this the spot?" I asked Kenya.

"Yeah, Kizzy ain't gon lie to me and just to be sure, I even came out here a couple of times by myself."

"Well, I'm just making sure cause shit bout to get too real." I said while double checking to make sure my Mac90 was locked and loaded. "You ready?"

"Waitin' on you." She said.

We both got out the car, leaving it running. The street was pitch black due to the street lights being busted. The only sound was the purr from the Nissan Altima I had rented and some dogs barking in the distance. Kenya took the left side while I took the right. After we carefully looked through all the windows we both came to the conclusion that there were only two people in the house. They were in the bed together sleep.

I aimed the Mac over the window and squeezed the trigger. Glass flew everywhere but it didn't stop me from completing my mission and making my point. When I felt satisfied I released the trigger but Kenya continued to unload her modified AR15. I had to touch her shoulder to break her out of her trance. When I looked inside, both occupants lay lifeless in the bed and blood was splattered all over the walls and carpet.

As we exited the yard, a couple neighbors dared to peek out of their windows. Kenya greeted them with a shower of bullets and they clearly got the message. We jumped back in the rental car and got far as possible from the crime scene.

A week had passed since somebody had attempted to take Mercedes's life. We all came to the conclusion that this Str8Drop beef had to come to an end. Within this week Jordan had killed several low ranking souljas just to send a message. Kizzy was officially apart of Queens Up and she played her role by getting the inside information from the nigga Jack. Although we couldn't pin-point where the nigga Peanut was at. Kizzy was able to get us info on where his baby mama and eight year old daughter stayed. I guess you know how that just went. That's how this game gets played from. Now on. These fuck niggas hide then I smoke their ass by getting at their family. Now all I gotta do is sit back and wait on this fuck nigga to come to me.

    I shut the spot down in Lincoln Field and had Kenya relocate to the North Miami Beach area. I dropped her back to the spot and told her to get rid of the guns, then I slid to check on Mercedes. The hospital had finally released her the day before and she was staying over at J.T's house until she got better. I personally couldn't stand J.T because he wouldn't stop cheating on Mercedes but I was comforted because I knew that he would never let nobody physically hurt my sister and he stayed in a secluded neighborhood. I at least gave him that much credit. When I pulled up to his house the clock in the Altima said 12:46am. J.T was sitting on the screened in porch smoking a black-n-mild.

"What's up J.T?" I said, opening the screen door.

"Shit, chilling what's up wit you?" he asked in his deep voice.

"Just another day" I said, "Where's Mercedes?"

"She in the house" he said, pointing with his head.

When I walked in the house and into J.T's bedroom Mercedes was in the bed counting some money and letting the TV watch her.

"Hoe what you doing over here?" she said.

"I came over here to check on you and makin sure I didn't have to kill J.T's ass."

"Nah, he good for now but if he get me wrong I will be calling you to come help get rid of his body." She said laughing.

"Did you get with the crime scene technician that I paid to get the finger prints off dad's chess board?"

"Yeah, she came by today and picked it up. She said she will call or come by in 48 hours with the results."

"Alright, well make yourself useful and go by the castle when you feel up to it and do some more digging. Break two of them bricks down into ounces cause I got some new custos I'm expecting to hit me up soon."

"Yeah, I'mma take care of that. So what's up with the streets and this Str8drop shit?" she asked.

"Me and Kenya just freed Peanut of a baby mamma and daughter so now the tables have turned and I'm sure he'll come lookin for us now, but I'll be ready when he comes."

"Damn hoe, yall killed the daughter too?"

"Bitch I don't pick faces when it come to my blood. Shit, if he don't show his face soon I'mma kill his momma, grandma, and dog too." I said dead serious.

Mercedes just shook her head. "Oh, what's the verdict on Neno?" she asked.

"Jordan just waitin' on the word but we ain't got no real evidence so he under investigation for now. I been so caught up with this Str8Drop shit that I ain't really had a chance to do my homework but thanks for reminding me."

"Yeah, I'mma do some snoopin' around since I can't do to much more than drive with this cast on my leg."

"Call me before you do anything Mercedes and make sure you be careful."

"Did you get the bullet proof vest?" she asked.

"Yeah, yours in the car, I'mma give it to J.T on my way out."

"Alright. But what happened at the meeting?"

"I put five more soulja on, relocated Kenya, put Neno on probation and promoted Jordan until you bounce back 100 percent. He in charge of the new souljas"

"Well excuse me I guess you got everything under control then" she said sarcastically.

"Yeah but I can't keep it up without you. I ain't slept a full eight hours since you got shot", I told herr, "but it's gettin late and I gotta drop this rental off so I'mma hit you up tomorrow. "

"Alright, I love you hoe, be safe."

"I will" I said as I got up and grabbed my keys.

"Don't forget to give J.T the vest for me" she said as I walked out of the room and then out of the house.

16

Peanut

"QUIET!"

The entire assembly of Str8Drop soldiers were immediately silenced as their leader positioned himself on the make shift stage.

"Can anybody in here tell me what the fuck Str8Drop stand for?!!" I asked all 62 of my souljas. I called a mandatory meeting because I was losing too many people beside the few that got themselves tangled up with the law, it seemed like somebody was working overtime to take my people out.

I'm the realist and the reality is that we all are aware of the possible consequences of gang bangin' so on that note I could rationalize somewhat. But when it came to my family that was another story. Two days ago I was called to positively identify the remains of my daughter and her momma. The truth of the matter is though, when I got to the scene there wasn't much of them that remained.

"Yeah," my souljas answered in unison.

"You" I pointed at the newest member I could spot, "What does Str8Drop stand for?!"

Just like he was trained, he stood to attention and said loud and clear, "Unity, discipline, never backin' down, doin' what's necessary for the family and overcoming self-gratification."

"So what the fuck seem to be the problem?" I screamed.

In the room there was a deadly silence as they all waited on me to continue. "We don't go around startin' problems but when they come we handle them. This beef with these hoes", I paused and let it sink in. "I want an end to this like yesterday! I ain't tellin y'all to start doing dumb shit and get caught up cause we don't move like that. In the past 8 months since that incident at Club Boulevard, I done lost 13 souljas, my baby momma, and my daughter. That shit is unacceptable and embarrassing to every last one of us. All y'all managed to do is shoot one of them!" Nobody dared to speak.

"I even got somebody working on the inside of they clique and y'all still can't stop these bitches?!" Still quiet. "I got 50 thousand in cash for the person who bring me them two sister hoes alive." I paused and looked around as I observed each of my crew members. "Meetin over!"

And everybody dispersed on a mission to get rich or die tryin.

17

Mercedes

"Listen Mercedes, I hope you don't mind me being professional about this, but Alexus paid me personally so I gotta give you what she paid for." She said. I just sat quiet as the crime scene technician pulled some papers from a big yellow envelope.

"Okay" she started after she had gotten herself situated at J.T's dining room table. "Latent prints are made when the natural oils and sweat present between the ridges of a person's fingertips are transferred to a surface by touch. Hard surfaces are usually dusted with finger print powder, which sticks to the traces of oil and sweat left on the object.

Powders come in different colors the crime scene technician chooses the powder that provides the most contrast with the object being dusted....."

I'm in love with dick but I had to give credit where it was due, this little educated red-bone bitch is bad. I'm glad J.T ain't here because I may have had to kill this hoe and that nigga.

"You following me?" she asked, bringing me back to reality.

"Yeah I'm listenin", I said, it wasn't a lie because my mind had only drifted towards the end.

She continued. "Fine carbon powder is used on light colored surfaces while aluminum powder reveals prints on dark surfaces and then a latent print lifting tape is applied. Even clothing and non-slick surfaces such as a paper can be examined, an iodine fuming method is required but it can be done."

"For real?" I asked, mainly to let her know that I was following her still.

"Yes, the item is placed in an enclosed cabinet with iodine crystals and then heated. The iodine vapor given off the crystals combined with traces of amino acids from human sweat left by the touch and we are able to pull prints from just about any surface." She was apparently done with her presentation, so I asked her about the results from the chess board and pieces.

"That is a very mysterious situation for me and I'm glad I didn't get hired to figure it out" she said pulling out a single paper from a separate envelope. "From almost every white chest piece, I retrieved your father's fingerprints. On the board itself were more finge and palm prints but all of them turned out to be your dad's as well. On the black chess pieces, there wasn't a single print, not even a partial one."

"That doesn't make sense" I said.

"That's the same thing I said. The way I see it is even if he had a long drawn out game by himself, why are his prints everywhere else except the black pieces? Then again, if he was playing somebody else why were they so careful to not touch the board and go through the hassle of cleaning the pieces?" she said.

I could tell that she was well trained and knew the boundary of her employment because she didn't wait on an answer. She gathered her belongings and waited to be escorted out to her car. Once she got inside of her 2014 Honda Accord she handed me her business card and told me that she could do all kinds of clean-ups for the right price, she winked her eye, closed the door and slowly backed out the driveway.

Curiosity eventually got the best for me and two hours later I found myself in route to the castle.

*"Niggas thought we was just about rappin'/and disrespected
Wonder what the fuck happened /When we hit they set*

Rippin' up the whole block in it ain't no stoppin'/ When them choppas get to choppin you get popped
Niggas crawlin, niggas boppin/Tryna get away from this "K"
I told you that we don't play..........."

Most people think that because I'm a hoe I'm supposed to listen to that Trina and Nicki Minaj but I fucks wit B.G., the old B.G you could hear the hunger in his voice and a certified gangsta could always get my pussy wet. I listened to B.G. as I cruised along the 45 minute trip to the castle.

My phone rung interrupting my vibe. "Hello?" I answered. Jordan was urgently screaming into my phone and I could barely made what he was saying. "Jordan calm down and tell me what's up." I screamed back in frustration.

"I'mma kill that fuck nigga Peanut" he said, "about an hour ago our new spot in Opa-Locka got shot up and two of our men got killed. I was supposed to be at the spot but just so happened that on my way Fantasy called me because he caught a flat tire on the turnpike."

"Damn" was all I could say. "Did you get the guns and dope out the spot?"

"Hell nah, when I got there the whole block was roped off. Shit, even the feds was on the scene."

"Alright, close down all the spots for today and get off the streets. Tell everybody I called a mandatory meeting at the Golden Corral restaurant in Homestead tomorrow at 4pm sharp and I'mma call Alexus myself so call me later. Be safe."

"Yeah you too" he said and the phone disconnected. So Peanut and his squad done finally bust back. The only problem with that is how the fuck they know where the new spot was at? It was just a stash spot and only a handful of people even knew that it existed. There was only one conclusion and it meant that somebody in Queens Up was playing both sides.

I dialed Alexus personal number but before the phone could ring, a thought intruded my thinking pattern and I hung up and called Jordan back. "Yeah?" he answered after the first ring.

"Change of plans," I told him "I need you to personally close down all the spots and tell everybody to take today and tomorrow off but be on standby for a mandatory meeting on Sunday."

"Where the meeting gon' be at?"

"I'll call everybody with instructions later. Just be safe and tell everybody to stay by their phones as usual."

"Alright, no problem." He said. "Oh and Mercedes....."

"Yeah?"

"Nice to have you back."

"Thanks J-Dubb but remember, you don't have to be on stage to be a part of the play."

I called Alexus and filled her in on my plans. I brought her up to date about the unfortunate deaths of our souljas and the financial losses we had to deal with. I also filled her in on the fingerprint results. There were too many unexplained occurrences and unanswered questions. I could almost smell the unmistakable and awful odor of defeat and dishonor. The worst part is that stink was coming from my clique.

18

Alexus

The animosity and hostility between Queens Up and Str8Drop had reached its orgasm. Peanut and his clique had turned the volume up and increased the pressure. They had turned the tables and modified the game. Instead of being on the offense we now had to defend our image, reputation, and more significantly our lives.

To add insult to injury, me and Mercedes were both convinced that one of our own was in bed, lying next to the enemy. Our roster had shrank in size since Str8Drop terminated two of ours in Opa-Locka the day before. Now Queens up consisted of me,

Mercedes, Jordan, Kenya, Neno , Kizzy, Torch, Dante, and Pharaoh. Mercedes made complete sense when she said that we had a disloyal informant in our ranks. She proposed and orchestrated schemes to bring light to the darkest betrayal of dishonor.

First, she gave Jordan orders to shut down all operations and inform the other members to be ready for a mandatory meeting between six and nine pm tomorrow. Mercedes planned to tell everybody to meet at different spots and then at the last second change the location. The way she saw it was if Str8Drop was trying to extinguish Queens Up then they would not pass up the opportunity to get us all in the same place at the same time.

After weighing the pros and cons I was supportive of her theory. If there was a snake in Queens Up, we would be able to determine who by whatever location was ambushed. Putting our heads together, we decided on having everybody meet up at Motel 6 in the isolated community of Coral Gables.

The plan was to meet at a room that only me and Mercedes would know about and tell everybody else that we would all meet at different room numbers. Me or Mercedes would then be in the front that room door when they arrived individually. One of us would personally walk them to our real meeting room, therefore if that person was the informant they would be unable to place any calls that would tip off the enemy to our change of plans.

    She assigned a room to each member of our clique. Jordan was given room 202 and was told to be there at 6pm. Kenya was told that we would meet at room 210 and urged to be there at 6:30 pm sharp. Neno was directed to report room 307 and was told to be there at 7:00pm, no earlier no later or that was his ass as far as Queens Up was concerned. Kizzy was given room 404 with instructions to be there at 7:30 pm. Torch was sent to room 421 at 8pm. Dante to room 501 at 8:30 and finally Pharaoh was ordered to be at room 516 at precisely 9pm.

We made the decision to not give anybody their room numbers until they called from their cars while pullin up to the hotel. That way they wouldn't speak amongst each other and peep our scheme. After planning, me and Alexus made our way to the motel so we could have everything in place for the next day. I got a room under one of my many aliases and we insisted that we get a room overlooking the parking lot entrance. We had a little resistance from the counter clerk but after a minor monetary bride and lil flirting, he was more than willing to supply me with the perfect room. For the next couple of hours me and Mercedes made strategic plans in order to shed some light on this fuck nigga or trifling bitch.

We placed our everyday vehicles, my 2014 hunter green Nissan Altima and Mercedes 2015 Chevy Impala in the parking lot to announce our presence. We also rented two 2015 Ford Taurus' and parked them close to the rear exit just in case.

After another small fee and seductive conversation, the counter clerk would let us know when each one of our members had arrived and would be on the lookout for suspicious activity. I made him a promise or two and sold him a few dreams, before I knew it he was a part of the grand scheme. I equipped him with a few Facebook pictures of who to expect and he was more than happy to play his role.

Then me and Mercedes went our separate ways because we had other shit to tend to. I ended up stopping by the Castle because shit was just not making sense to me. Mercedes had told me all about the fingerprinting results and shit just wasn't adding up.

Once I pulled up to the castle the sun was just setting. I saw Ms. Gloria pulling out as I was pulling in and we exchanged a little small talk. She was off to run a few errands and she offered to make dinner if I was gone be a while. I was and Ms. Gloria could work miracles in the kitchen so I was looking forward to dinner.

I went through the process of the high tech security and straight to dad's den that housed the secret rooms. I was curious as to who would my dad have been playing chess with and why were they so careful as to wipe their fingerprints from the chess pieces?

In room number 2 where the notebook was with all dad's contacts, I flipped through page after page not really knowing what I was supposed to be looking for. Only thing that stuck out to me more than the judges, lawyers, and FBI agent names was the mention of this dude named Devin. So much had went on since I last made the mental note to check on Devin that it had totally slipped my mind. Why the fuck did dad go through so much trouble to investigate this Devin dude so carefully?

After I closed up downstairs I moved upstairs to the camera room. I could tell mom had been there because there was a slightly cooled Diet coke sitting on the table leaving a wet ring. I could also smell the faint scent of her signature White Diamond perfume. On the cameras home computer I go to the week before my dad died. I didn't know what I was looking for specifically so I put the recording on fast forward and watched the entrance gate. I wanted to know if dad had any visitors and if so who were they?

    Come to find out, dad had plenty visitors it seemed like all the time. Everything from Bentleys to Range Rovers pulled up and was granted access to the Castle. It wasn't hard to find out who they were because dad was persistent at keeping logs and in the security office there was a file cabinet specifically for logging time, dates, names and license plate numbers of people who entered and exited the gates of the castle.

    After what seemed like an hour and a half. Ms. Gloria's car was shown on the live camera pulling back into the castle and minutes later she was calling my phone and telling me that dinner would be ready in about a half an hour. The time on my phone read 9:45pm and I figured I would use the next 30 minutes to do more research.

I checked each vehicle out carefully as I watched them enter and exit the castle and I made notes to do research on just about all of them. Just as I got ready to wrap it up for the night, my attention was drawn to a silver Nissan Altima that pulled into the sally port and then when denied access to the castle, the car eased back and drove off. I was suspicious because dad's house was in a secluded neighborhood and nobody just makes a mistake arriving at the castle. As I rewound and replayed the footage over a couple times, I could barely see a silhouette of a person in the driver's seat. The person in the car reached his or her hand out the driver's window and tried to gain access to the castle using their finger print. When denied, they left.

Who the fuck could that have been? I was sure that they were unannounced and unexpected. If not, then dad would have made sure they were allowed in. Why hadn't they just waited and called to gain access? None of this made any logical sense to me.

I immediately dialed Kenniesha's number. She had done a professional job with fingerprinting the chess board and she was talking reasonable prices. I had come across her number in the notebook for dads connects and contacts. Kenniesha is a crime scene technician and she makes extra money by using the equipment at work for her benefit. She had a team that cleaned up blood spills off the record. Kenniesha ran and matched DNA samples and could even perform autopsies. At face value you would assume that she was an ordinary working female, but when money was on the table she knew how to get it. Kenniesha was what Queens

Up needed and would play an important role, if she was willing to commit and I made up my mind to give her a position on the team when the time was right.

"Hello?" she answered, sounding as though I was interrupting her sleep.

"My bad if I woke you up, it's me Alexus"

Her voice sounded alert instantly. "Nah, you stopped my show a little bit but he can wait."

"Oh shit, I'm sorry." I said embarrassed. "I'll call you tomorrow."

"Trust me girl, I can get dick any day but money makes me cum." She said boldly. "So what's up?"

"Well, look I'm at my dad's house doing my homework and I ran across some suspicious looking shit on the surveillance cameras like a week before he died. The thing is I can't zoom in close enough to see what I am interested in clearly. Can you help me with that?"

"I'mma be real with you, that ain't my area of expertise but I got some dudes who are fucking computer gurus! They're expensive though and they can be real busy at times. I know money ain't no issue with you but I don't know how long you can wait, I'll definitely give him a call ASAP."

"Shit I do appreciate it Kenniesha and as long as he can have it done in a reasonable amount of time then you can go ahead and let him know that I got money on deck and up front. I got a little something for you too.

"Well let me finish scratching my itch and you can just email me the video."

I got the email information from her and let her go. I made me a copy of the video and sent it to my email and forwarded it to Kenniesha. I cleaned up the office and followed my nose to the kitchen where Ms. Gloria was in the process of putting food on plates. She made some curry chicken, yellow rice, broccoli, and garlic butter biscuits. I washed my hands and sat at the table. She brought the plates out and then went to retrieve a chilled bottle of kiwi Moscato champagne. We ate and discussed future plans for the both of us. She expressed her loneliness at the castle and wondered why me and Mercedes or mom didn't move in yet. I could see the longing in her eyes, she was use to planning parties, catering and being needed. She even expressed how she felt that she didn't earn the $100,000 dollars a year that dad left her in his will. We chatted till about midnight before I made my way to my hide out.

Truth is I identified with Ms. Gloria's feelings of loneliness because I hadn't had a serious relationship for about 6 years. It's not that I wasn't attractive because I'm approached by men all the time. The thing is that I don't trust many people. In my past I've been used and abused, mistreated and unappreciated. I cast my pearls before swine and in return been shitted on. I grew tired of giving niggas power over my emotions and instead of looking for love, I decided to let it find me. Even the few niggas that I dated over the last couple of years couldn't keep up with me. My million dollar body and million dollar mind made niggas nervous to be around me. It ain't my fault that I ran circles around these fuck niggas.

Entering my condo on South Beach feeling the effects of the champagne, I undressed leaving a trail of clothing from the front door to my bathroom and turned the Jacuzzi water on. I added some Victoria Secret Mango Rush bathing gel to the water and watched the Jacuzzi fill with bubbles. I turned the lights dim and stepped in the 98 degree water, then I eased down and allowed myself to be submerged in the provocative smelling bath.

After a few minutes I reached over to the bathroom cabinet and retrieved my 9 inch double penetration, aluminum dildo. I lifted one of my legs over the side of the tub and inserted the dildo in my pussy nice and slow. I wasn't in no rush and while closing my eyes I grinded my hips and pleasured myself. After a couple of relaxed strokes, I gained speed and felt myself explode in the mango scented water. I layed my head back and relaxed while feeling the rush of my orgasm. I wanted to go for round two but I allowed the pains of business to penetrate my thoughts of pleasure. Truth be told, I was worn out and needed a small break from it all to recuperate. The sad part is that I knew it was impossible to ride the bench at this time in the game of my life.

By the time I got out the tub the bathroom clock said 1:43 am and I felt my body shutting down from fatigue. I dried off, lotion up and made my way to the confines of my lonely king sized canopy bed. I set my alarm for 10am and before my head hit the pillow I had already drowned in the black abyss of unconsciousness.

The next day or better yet when day came, I was awaken by the sound of Beyoncé coming from my personal phone. Without opening my eyes, I answered it. "Damn, you not up yet?" Mercedes asked because she heard the sleep in my voice.

"Nah, what time is it?" I asked.

"Almost one o'clock in the afternoon" she said.

I opened my eyes in shock and checked the time on my phone, sure enough it was 12:47pm "Damn, I don't know how I didn't hear my alarm, but I'm up now, what's up?"

"Shit meet me at the Motel 6 at 4pm, ain't too much of shit else going on. I already made the rounds and did our inventory at the spots, then called and did roll call for the clique everybody's accounted for." She said.

"Alright I'm getting up now and I'll see you at four."

I hung up with Mercedes and climbed out of the comforts of my Martha Stewart blanket. I placed my feet on the floor and sat on the edge of the bed. I reached over to my nightstand for my bible and performed my daily ritual of reading Psalms 35. After reading and meditating over all 28 verses, I said a small prayer.

I got up and brushed my teeth, took a quick shower and made a cup of instant coffee. When I was situated and ready to start business I checked my business phone. All operations were shut down so I didn't expect many calls. The only call I had was from Kenniesha at 9am. She had also sent an email asking me to call her when I got the chance. I went to her name in the phone and hit the call button.

She answered on the second ring sounding like her day was in mid stride. "Hey Alexus, what's up?"

"Shit, I'm just starting my day. Sorry I missed your call."

"You good but anyways, I hit my people up about the video and he assured me that he would be able to zoom in as much as possible." she said.

"Alright cool. Did you send him the video that I emailed to you?"

"You didn't give me permission or instructions to forward the video and I don't move like that."

"That's what I like to hear."

"Yeah, I'm content with following orders and I only give them when I'm runnin' the show. But this yo' show so...."

"So, what numbers he asking to complete the job?"

"He owe me a few favors so consider this a gift and as soon as he done with his current project, which should take about 3 more days, he will get on the job."

I laughed, "Sound like you making decisions and giving orders to me."

She laughed, "Well I'm at work so let me go and act busy."

"Alright girl, I'll catch you later. Hit me up if you need something and thanks."

"I'll hold you to that and you're welcome." She said. We said our goodbyes and hung up.

The clock on my phone said 2:30pm, I started to get my things together in preparation to leave the house and make it to the Motel by 3:30. I cleaned my glock 40 and grabbed the Tek 9 as well. I put on my Nike Air Max sneakers and my Apple Bottom Jeans, placed my guns and extra ammo inside of my Louis Vuitton book bag and headed to the Dodge Charger that I rented for this occasion.

I made it to the Motel at 3:28pm and did a survey of the parking lot. I rode by my Nissan Altima and Mercedes' Chevy Impala to see if anything looked out of place. Then I rode by the two Ford Taurus' to do the same. I scanned the parking lot from the safety of the car and watched for any people lingering around or looking suspicious. When I got next to this champagne gold Dodge Intrepid, I saw somebody just sitting in the driver's seat with the seat reclined.

QUEEN'S UP

Then my phone rang.

19

Mercedes

"Hello?" My sister answered.

"Hoe, where you at?" I asked.

"I'm already at the Motel just peepin' out the surrounding."

"Yea me too, you see that Black Dodge Charger creepin' through the parking lot?" I asked.

"Yeah, that's me. Where you at?"

"I'm in the gold Dodge Intrepid."

"Oh shit, I'm sittin' here feelin' some type of way bout the Intrepid and that's yo' dumb ass", she said.

"Shit I was about to dump at the motherfuckin Charger if it crept pass me one more time."

"Everything good out here then so meet me in the room." She said, then hung up.

I watched Alexus back as she made her way to the Motel entrance. I was feeling back to normal beside the occasionally thump pain in my leg every now and again. Against the doctor's wishes I had the cast taken of my leg because I couldn't be on the sideline cheering while my team was on the battle field.

After 20 minutes, I made my way in the hotel. Without glancing up to the room window I knew that Alexus was watching my back the whole way. I greeted the overly eager desk clerk as he tried his best to suppress a blush. I know Alexus got away with her words but I wonder what dream she sold him.

Instead of taking the elevator to the 6th floor took my time and climbed the stairs. You could tell that the stairs were rarely used and probably only by the house keepers and maintenance staff. I was basically just looking at all of our exit routes in case shit got out of hand.

At 4:13pm I used my electronic access card to open the door to room 666. The irony hit me as I closed the door and I wondered who would be taking the trip to visit the devil tonight. I could smell the thick scent of coffee that Alexus was sipping at the room's table. She had her laptop open looking at the hidden surveillance cameras that we had in the parking lot on the two rental cars and our personal vehicles. We also placed hidden cameras at the rear exit doors. She briefed me on her research at the castle and our next major investment. We discussed potential soldiers because we had 8 keys of the purest and it was time to expand.

Gustavo was a decent supplier and we still purchased cocaine from him at our regular times and in our regular quantities. We thought of Gustavo as a stepping stone but we didn't need bad blood between us at this point, in the game plus we were in a win win situation.

We talked until 5:55 pm when Jordan called my cell phone. "Yeah?" I answered.

"I'm runnin 5 minutes late, but what's the room number?" he asked.

"Room 202 Jordan, and park next to my Impala in the front."

"Alright, I can smoke in there right?"

"Yeah boy just hurry up, bye." I said and ended the call without waiting on a response.

Two minutes later I watched Jordan's 2013 Nissan Maxima ease in the parking lot. Instead of parking next to my Impala he cruised through the parking lot, doing what me and Alexus had done when we first got there. We lost sight of his car but as he went around the rear of the Motel the rental cars hidden camera picked him up and then he reappeared in the front and parked next to my car.

At 6:03pm he exited his vehicle and at 6:07pm he was standing in front of room 202 where Alexus met him then walked him to our room. Jordan ain't no dumb nigga and even though he ain't say shit his nonchalant distance told me that he was feeling played by being told the wrong room number. I can't blame him, I would've felt the same way too but this wasn't a time for feelings. I was taught the dangerous disadvantages of thinking with feeling and how I felt right now my life was almost taken and my back was against the wall.

At 6:20pm I watched out the window as Kenya's 2010 Maroon colored Nissan Altima penetrated the entrance of the Motel's parking lot. She didn't call before she parked and I didn't want to call and tip her off that she was being watched. Alexus exited the room, leaving me and Jordan. I watched Kenya climb out of her car and walk around the Motel's building acting as if she was on the phone. I knew her well enough to know that she was executing her own perimeter check. Instead of coming through the entrance, she walked through the rear exit. And at 6:32pm, her and Alexus strolled through the doors of our hotel's suite.

"I know you hoes didn't just try me like that?" Kenya said, clearly pissed the fuck off.

"I ain't got nothing to do with this" Jordan said, "I just got here at 6."

"Y'all might as well get the fuck out y'all feelings and understand that this business and I'mma need you to put yo' cell phone next to Jordan's on that table." Alexus told her.

In Kenya's face I could read the disgust but she did as told fell back on the bed grabbed the remote and flipped the channels of the muted 57 inch plasma that hung on the wall. At 6:50pm Neno's navy blue 2013 Charger SRT slid on the grounds of the Motel. He got out of his car immediately and unlike the rest of us he walked right into the hotel's lobby

I'm going to go meet him." Alexus said, looking pissed.

"I'm going with you." Jordan said, putting his .45 caliber Smith and Wesson on his waist. Then they both walked out the door. A couple seconds later the hotel's room phone rang.

"Hello?" I asked.

"Ma'am it's the guy from the picture. He asked what room you were in and I didn't want to seem suspicious so I sent him to the room that he was supposed to go to, uh.....room 307," The clerk said.

"Good job being on point, I'll make sure you get something extra for that." I told him and heard him giggle like a little school kid. Then I disconnected the call. Three minutes later, Jordan, Neno and Alexus walked in the room and you could feel the tension. As soon as the door closed and Alexus locked it up, Jordan pulled his out gun and let it hang at his side. We all saw the blood in Jordan's eyes and chose to remain quiet, even Kenya.

"Neno no disrespect this just business." Alexus said.

"What the fuck you talking about, what's going on?" Neno asked.

Jordan cocked his gun back. "Listen Neno speak when requested and follow directions and we won't have no problems." Neno reluctantly obeyed, really not having a choice and Jordan went directly for his waist removing his 9mm pistol and passed it back to me. He then went in his pocket, removed his wallet, cell phone, and car keys. I put them all on the table with the rest of everybody's shit.

"Now get naked." Jordan demanded.

"Huh?" Neno asked while looking at Kenya who just shrugged her shoulders.

"What the fuck? You think I'm playin?" Jordan barked. Neno didn't respond verbally, he just started to come out of his shirt, revealing his nicely sculpted chest. Then took off his Levi's and was left standing in Polo boxers and socks.

"Come up out that shit." Jordan said. He took off his socks and then his boxers. Jordan checked his clothes like he was performing a jail house strip search then piece by piece he threw them back at Neno to get dressed. Neno, looking defeated, grabbed a chair from the table and put it in a corner and sat there quietly putting on his socks and shoes.

"All you had to do was follow directions and call from the parking lot Neno." I told him, but he didn't respond.

At 7:25 pm Kizzy was calling from the parking lot. I was expecting to see her champagne gold Cadillac STS but she hopped out of a white Audi A8 with a paper tag. Alexus told her to go to room 404 and she and Kenya went to meet her. About 5 minutes later they came in the room laughing. The fact that she did her best not to look at Neno gave away the reason they were all humored. Without giving any instructions Kizzy immediately placed her phone and purse on the table and then shocked us all by unzipping and coming out of her pants, then her shirt. She didn't stop there she took off her Victoria's Secret matching lace bra and panty set. She ain't have no complex and showed nothing but comfort on her face.

"Yall want me to bend over, squat and cough too?" she asked, while looking each of us in the eye.

"Girl you is crazy" Kenya said laughingly.

At 8:00pm Alexus and Kizzy went to meet Torch who had pulled up in a burnt orange 2015 Chevy Camaro. He called from the parking lot as instructed and was led to the room without incident.

Torch was a laid back but vicious kind of nigga. He didn't speak too loud or too much but when he spoke, you could feel the power and seriousness behind every word. His wardrobe never changed and it wasn't a day that you would see him outside of his signature American Eagle apparel. He stayed on his white boy swag and even though he was black like Morris Chestnut or Akon, he could blend in with the hood niggas or the preppy college kids.

"Damn yall don't trust me or somthin?" he asked while looking at all of us as he came through the door. Neno pointed at the table and without missing a beat Torch took his phone and wallet out of his pocket sat it on the table then went in his other pocket and came out with his keys.
"Book bag" Jordan said.

"Oh, yeah" he said, then took his Gucci book bag off his back, unzipped it and dumped the contents on the bed. A Tek 9, 2 clips and three stacks of money wrapped in rubber bands.

Me, Alexus, Jordan, Kenya, Kizzy, Neno and Torch chatted for a while, while waiting for Dante and Pharaoh to show up. Within the group I was the one that basically sat back and watched the movements and expressions of all the members. Everybody was their normal selves, even Neno had finally got out of his feelings and joined in on the conversation. Phones were ringing but they were all going unanswered even mine and Alexus only answered her phone when Dante called.

"Yeah?" she answered and put the phone on speaker so we all could hear.

"I'm like 5 minutes away but I'm stopping at the gas station, you need anything?" he asked.

"Yeah get me a cranberry juice and get Mercedes a strawberry flavored Smirnoff."

"Yall the only two there?" he asked and alerted all 6 senses at once.

"Yeah" she said and I stood up to look out the window.

"What room yall in?" he asked.

"We in room 501, now hurry up cause you already late", she hung up the phone.

"Torch, Kenya and Kizzy y'all come with me", she said authoratively and exited the room.

Ten minutes later they all returned including Dante and I could tell that Alexus was pissed because

I saw the same look in her eyes that I saw that night at the hospital.

"Put all ya shit on the table Dante" Torch said as he locked the door.

"What's goin on?" Dante asked.

"Just do it", Jordan told him, "and while you're at it, get naked."

"Stop fucking trying me." Dante said.

"I advise you to do what the fuck he just told you to do." Neno warned.

After scanning the room and feeling the tension, Dante took off his Jordan's first, then his True Religion jeans and Polo shirt. He was left standing in his boxers, socks and polo wife beater.

"Come up out that shirt" Neno said redirecting his own embarrassment.

Alexus' phone rang and I answered it because I could tell that her mind had crossed over to a land consumed with fire breathing dragons or some shit. All rights reserved. Without limiting the rights under copyright reserved. No part of this book may be reproduced, stored in any or introduced into a retrieval system, to transmitted in any form, or by any means (Electronic, mechanical, photocopying, recording, or otherwise), without prior written consent from both the author and the publisher, except for the brief quotes that are used in literary reviews.

"Go to room 516 and thank you for being on time." I told him.

Kenya and I walked to meet him. We met him coming out the elevator and pushed him back in, then we took the quick ride up from the 5th to the 6th floor. Pharaoh was clearly confused but he wise and remained quiet. When we got in the room he reluctantly and without the slightest hesitation placed his keys, wallet, .357 magnum Smith and Wesson, couple gold magnum condoms and some purple haze on the table and sat down on the edge of the bed.

We all sat quietly as Alexus calmly went inside her Louis Vuitton book bag and pulled out her chrome glock 40 and clicked the safety off. "Look" she started making sure he had all of our attention. "A couple of y'all got this shit twisted. When it comes to Queens Up, I run this shit. When its Queens Up business that means you on my time. Before you became a part of this circle, I had to give the okay. Just because I don't push my weight around don't mean that I ain't in control. Neno, just because I ain't got in your chest don't think I don't know about you selling loud out my trap. Dante the next time you deviate when you on my time, I'm gone come see bout you. And Pharaoh, my motherfcking trap ain't no hoe house so you need to tighten up. Take that as a warning. Now the reason Mercedes called this meeting is because we convinced that somebody playing both sides." She paused as everybody looked around at each other. I just sat watching the surveillance cameras from the laptop.

"Yeah that's right", she continued, "and when I find out who it is, I'mma kill yo whole family. Don't think that because I got a pussy between my legs that its pussy in my heart. If you ain't the snake then this don't apply to you, but if you is the reporting to that fuck nigga Peanut then let him know that his baby momma and his daughter was just the beginning and this shit don't end until I kill the head. Just some advice for the wise. If you remaining loyal to Queens Up I'mma take you to the top but if you get out the car, you gone get ran the fuck over."

After Alexus got through addressing the squad, I took the spotlight. "I ain't got much more to add except that we pulling in numbers collectively and the only thing slowing us down is the Str8Drop beef. Listen, if you can't handle the pressure then just walk away now and it is what it is. But when the light shed on the disloyalty, I'mma back my sister up the whole way. For the last two days we had to shut down operation, we done missed out on about 150 racks. I watched as everybody eyes got big.

"Yeah, shit if we can expand and some more loyal souljas we'll make that back and more. Being that it's 10:30pm and I ain't got the call I was looking for. I'm going to assume that everyone in this room on the same page but one slip up and shit going get stupid ugly. From now on its three strikes you're out. Dante, you got one more strike for deviating from the instructions, Neno, one more strike and you're out for deviating and having company at my spot in Perrine, not to mention that other shit we unclear about. From this point on all rules are to be followed and any deviations will be disciplined accordingly."

We all talked among each other while Alexus doubled checked the desk clerk for any report of suspicious activity. He must have said that everything was normal because at 11:00pm Alexus gave everybody their new posts and positions and sent everyone on their way.

Jordan and Torch walked everybody to their cars and one by one we exited the parking lot in all different directions. I gave Pharaoh and Dante directions to return to the Motel the next day and return the two rental cars then park me and Alexus' cars at the spots where they were stationed.

20

Kenya

As everybody abandoned the Motel's parking lot in different directions, I lingered and leaned on the trunk of my Altima, kicking it with Torch. It was evident that me and Torch had grown mutual feelings for each other bordering affection but passed the stages of curiosity. We made plans to get together and get a bite to eat whenever our schedules permitted. We said our awkward see you later. I stood there for maybe a second too long and watched Torch swag to this Chevy Camaro. One hand holding his Gucci book bag and the other clutching his Tek 9.

Using my alarm pad, I unlocked my car door and got in the driver's seat. I put my purse in the passenger's seat while at the same time starting the engine. Then I reached for my seat belt and that's when I noticed the unfamiliar scent. I couldn't place the scent but I was damn sure it didn't belong. I felt the presence of a person behind me and the hairs on my body raised to attention. I fought for mental control and forced myself to remain ordinarily calm as I reached under the passenger seat for my .380. Before I could locate my gun, I felt the deadly cold steel of a gun barrel pressed against my head.

"I advise you to pay attention to every word and follow every direction or your mom, your two kid brothers and yourself are going to be cremated alive one after the other in that order." He said in a calm and calculated manner.

I was confused because I was expecting to hear the slang of a goon but this was the unmistakable dialect of a cracka in my back seat. "What you want from me?" I asked with some sense of authority trying to mask my fears.

"First I want you to pass me that purse."

"This about money? Listen how much you need? Maybe I can make that happen and then we can both be on our way." I felt the excruciating pain from being hit in the back of the head with the gun. My eyes began to tear as I fought not to black out.

"See that's what happens when you don't follow directions." He said, still in his calm voice.

I passed him my purse and a second later my phone rang.

"Here answer this and put it on speaker phone, then tell your little boyfriend that you are fine and make sure you insist that he leave. If you fail to get the message across and he comes this way, he and his car are going to look like Swiss cheese." He said, then handed me the phone.

I answered the phone and put it on speaker, "What's up Torch?"

"Shit, I'm waiting on you to pull out. Everything straight down there?"

"Boy I'm grown and I ain't never had a daddy. Trust I can take care of myself. You better get to the spot before Alexus start trippin'." I told him, trying not to give no signs of my current situation away.

"Damn you ain't gotta be so feisty" he replied. "Well let me get on my mission because I don't need the Queen in my chest or on my trail."

"I'mma most likely be tied up for the rest of the night trying to play catch up but I'mma hit you up in the a.m."

"Alright drive safe Kenya."

"You too" I said and the lines were disconnected. I heard the powerful engine of Torch's Chevy Camaro exiting the parking lot.

"Good job" the voice behind me said, not asking for a response and not getting one in return.

A second or two later a black Suburban pulled into the parking lot beside my car.

"Now take your seatbelt off and exit the vehicle and for your own good don't do anything stupid." I exited my Altima and waited on my next command. Without warning, the rear door of the 2015 Suburban was opened and I was shoved inside. Once inside the vehicle I was worn four white men and the one that was in my backseat got in the front seat of my car, reversed from the parking spot and pulled off heading in the direction of the parking lot exit. We followed close behind. I battled to remain calm and not speak unless I was spoken to.

I could feel the powerful aura of authority seeping through the pores of my abductors and no one spoke as we merged into the thinly spaced traffic of route I-75. I was expecting this situation to be connected with our Str8Drop beef but this felt like a completely different animal. Out of my peripheral I looked around for signs of some kind of law enforcement paraphernalia, slightly preferring to be apprehended by the Feds than the mafia.

Finally after 15 minutes of complete silence the passenger opened a manila folder and read from a file. "Kenya Lashawn Patterson, born May 11th 1990 to a Debra Patterson, father unknown. Immediate family consist of you and your two brothers, Brandon age 16 and Rodney age 17." He said, while handing back a picture of my momma in a dimly lit room tied to a chair and a picture of my brothers handcuffed to a restraint table in some type of cabin or barn.

I couldn't make out a word even if I wanted to, the air had been snatched away from my lungs as tears penetrated the confines of my eyelids, escaping like a few anxious prisoners. Then he continued to speak: "I'm not a religious person, truth be told, I think that I am God, but I heard in that book of deceit, lies and manipulation called the Holy Bible that life and death lies in the power of the tongue. Well, the lives of your family and maybe even yourself will depend on your tongue so from this point on choose your words wisely. As a matter of fact we'll play a game. Every time I ask you a question and you lie to me, you'll lose a body part starting with fingers then toes."

Then he turned around from the front passenger seat and asked, "Do you get the picture?" I nodded my head, still unable to speak. "Good, good" he said, "so you'll determine your own consequences", he turned around, lit a Cuban cigar and let his window down about an inch.

An hour and a half later, we passed the last exit south before entering the one way road to Key West. I was confused to say the least but after getting a taste of pain from being hit in the head, I thought it wise to keep my questions, comments and suggestions to myself. At 2:15am we entered what looked like a farm with a barn and two trailer homes, but not an animal insight.

"Get out!" the guard who sat on my left side that hadn't said a word the entire 3 hour drive ordered. They escorted me to the first trailer, inside was more spacious and exquisitely decorated than most cribs in the middle class neighborhoods. I was led through a formal living room, an antiquely furnished dining room, to a door that led to an underground chamber or some shit.

That's when my body froze and I couldn't persuade myself to walk into my own death. The four guards grabbed me and damn near dragged me down the short flight of stairs, my feet banged against the concrete steps until I fell face first on the dirt floor of a barely lit room. For my disobedient reluctance, I was rewarded by being pinned down on the floor and handcuffed, then helped to my feet just to be shoved down into a worn out chair in the middle of the basement.

There was a low ceiling filled with dust and spider webs, it dripped some kind of brown liquid that carried the unmistakable scent of fecal matter. There was a row of about three support beams that ran along the outer edge of the basement, they extended into the deep shadows on both sides of the room.

"Don't move out of that chair for no reason at all" was the order given before the four of them marched back up the stairs and out of the dungeon. I was left in this empty rat infested space and expected not to move, I understood that I was being watched though I didn't see the cameras. Maybe I was being tested to see if playing a whole lot of mind tricks and I didn't know how long I could withstand or if I had another fucking option.

"What the fuck do you want from me?!!" I screamed.

"To be tortured.....? Interrogated....? Am I going to die...?" Everything was left to my imagination and I'm more than sure that was the purpose.

They left me there my hands still cuffed behind my back for what felt like about four hours when the sun fought the moon for position and the sky transitioned from jet black to an early morning blue. Then the door opened. The guard who considered himself to be God descended the stairs followed by an elderly woman. She looked to be close to 80 years old and was helped down the stairs after growing faint. The guard accompanying her brought a chair and sat it about 5 feet in front of me.

"If you even breathe the wrong way you will die a very slow and agonizing death" she said in the calmest manner. She was helped into the chair and given a wool blanket to keep her frail body warm. "Thank you baby" she said as he turned around and sat on the stairs with his assault rifle pointed at me. "I was once your age" she began and then paused as if trying to conjure up her thoughts, "and I ran with the same kinds of circles, but the difference is we lived by morals. Y'all young people these days ain't got no respect, no values, and no sense of honor. Y'all think that violence is the answer to everything" she said while shaking her head in disagreement. "Young lady do you play chess?"

Huh? "Uh..no ma'am."

"See... 62 years ago when I was 21 years old my first husband introduced me to the game of chess. Ten years later I grew into a master chess player and even gave him a run for his money. When I fully understood the strategies of chess and applied those strategies to the affairs of my life, I evolved from a pawn to a Queen. I used my pawns wisely and never underestimated their value. While I at all times protected my king. My king is my money, my property, my honor and my integrity." Then she paused as if trying to catch her breath and after about a minute she continued. "Ms. Kenya Lashawn Patterson don't be flattered as if you are the center of my attention, because you are not. You are nothing more than a pawn that I will use to capture Alexus and Mercedes. In my opinion they were fine young women and I even admired their entrepreneurial skills. That is until they decided to play detective. Sampson was my baby, the only one that I was able to have until them pigs took him away from me."

When she referred to a white person as a "pig" I subconsciously looked over her shoulder to where the white guard was sitting with his assault rifle aimed at me. She didn't miss a beat. "See how simple minded you kids are these days? A white man or black man is not defined by his physical complexion but by the colors of his thoughts. When I was growing up most of the "crackers" were black'ah than me and you put together. Just like a nigga, they was given a little more table scraps and they sold their souls to the slave owners. When I gave birth to Sampson they stripped him away from me. By the time I escaped and tracked him down, he was well developed, married and never even knew that I existed. But I played the shadows and stayed close by as I built my own empire. I watched him rise and elevate to a man of an extremely high caliber. My son was successful and behind the scenes I gave myself a standing ovation when he brought Alexus and Mercedes into this world." She took a moment to catch her breath.

"He died not because of envy or jealousy but because he was disloyal and dishonest, and for that, I would've killed him myself. But after a year and a half I'll be damned if I let these hoes uncover my sons shame." She paused, clearly agitated and said, "You can stay here uncuffed and be treated like a half decent human being or you can stay here in chains but either way you will not leave here until Alexus, Mercedes, and the rest of Queens Up comes looking for you and fall right into my trap." She then snapped her fingers and the guard came and removed the wool blanket and helped her up the stairs where she was intercepted by another guard.

He came back down the stairs to uncuff me. "You'll stay here and if you cooperate, I will eventually bring your mom and your brothers to stay here with you. Remember what happens the first time you lie. I'll be back with food in a little while, the bathroom is there," he pointed to a door on my right that was slightly opened and it's only piece of furniture was an orange mop bucket. "There's a room with a mattress", he pointed to a small closet deep in the shadows of the room. "If I had my way you'd sleep and use the bathroom in that chair, so I'm praying that you mess this up." He said then walked up the stairs and out of the basement.

To be continued. ....

About the Author

CITY BOY 4RM DADE

FICTION/STREET LIT

Born into the roughest neighborhoods in Miami City, CityBoy had to get drug through the mud to make it to Paradise. Raised as a savage, he made the conscious decision to convert to Islam, where principles, values, and integrity molded him into a successful man. Recognizing that he had a story to tell, mixed with a level of intelligence, he set out to be the best.

DON'T FORGET TO FOLLOW SOULJA CHOC PRESENTS ON:

Facebook: SouljaChocPresentz

https://www.facebook.com/souljachocpresentz

Facebook Page: SouljaChocPresents2u

https://www.facebook.com/souljachocpresents2u/

Instagram: @SouljaChocPresents

https://www.instagram.com/souljachocpresents/

Twitter: @Soulja_Presents

https://twitter.com/soulja_presents

Web:

https://www.souljachocpresentsbooks.com/

Email:

souljachocpresents@gmail.com

Made in the USA
Columbia, SC
26 June 2023